Growing up on the east-side of Vancouver BC in the 60s there was no internet, no computer games; just pinball, and, by the mid-70s, Pacman, so we were to make our own games or play board games, which we did. We also did stupid things when it got boring like dekes where we would run down a crowded street and try not to hit anyone. Jail tag on bikes. As I got older, I started to read about WWII but it got boring so I began reading horror and science fiction.

To my son and family

Liam B. Dei

The Web

Austin Macauley Publishers™
London • Cambridge • New York • Sharjah

A CIP catalogue record for this title is available from the British Library.

ISBN 9781528913720 (Paperback)
ISBN 9781528919562 (ePub e-book)

www.austinmacauley.co.uk

First Published 2024
Austin Macauley Publishers Ltd®
1 Canada Square
Canary Wharf
London
E14 5AA

Braedon W. F. Dei

Prologue

I am a warrior, as I look over my homeland, I am reminded of a song of our father's, and a time of stability, in the constellation of planets. The destiny of all worlds in our system, though each one unique by stages of evolution, cannot exist without protection.

Enigma

Enigma
You ask why
Like the moon at dusk
Or a dawning sky

A wish
Or a spell that binds
A dish
As thoughts intertwine

Answer this
With each kiss
Is there solace
When received

An evening gown
Torn inside out
And believe, in the
Thought
Once perceived

And I thought
You would know
So I ask
Where to go
Mirroring looking in
As we search
Within
Where to begin

The forces of nature and the changes, occurring in the suns, that surround the central planets and their orbit, as they near the paradox, are now beginning to feel the changes as the blue star moves closer to their place in the universe. The pull of its gravity, its temperature, and UV's unique to the blue star, are causing global catastrophic happenings that are undeniable. Changes in atmospheric pressures, sunsets are becoming more brilliant, storms more severe and global volcanic eruptions from dead or extinct volcanoes, come to life without warning. I come from the most inner world.

We are the most advanced of all the planets and have created a type of grid that does not replace the OZONE but enhances it. It strengthens and protects our planet from UV's, produced by the Blue Star that is harmful. And we are just discovering other incredible and unbelievable uses of this grid. I am a part of a new generation of policing diplomat's that are responsible for integrating the rest of the planets.

Though not as advanced as ours, together under this new technology, we can and must protect them from annihilation.

The blue star syndrome is a recurring solar phenomenon that, every one-hundred-thousand millennium, gives enough time for a species, on each planet, to evolve to a level of intelligence and is then destroyed by the returning blue star. Because it generates so much heat and unknown UV rays it wipes out everything that was, with no records or architecture to give any consideration to existence or happenings.

By using the assaulting light, we can ascend to descend ourselves onto any planet in our system and interact with its occupants, study them and find our way into their order of structure and add our life skills. As we do this we find areas, predetermined by circumference and magnetic anomalies, and gravitational differences of force, where we can set monoliths in certain identified magnetic and gravitational fractures discovered by the two polar placements and the first six monoliths.

We count our planetary orbits as rotations, by fixing star patterns. I am on my 273rd life rotation, being a part of the assaulting light we, light streamers, live longer lives than most species. I am only one-quarter of my life's time, or a recorded, rotation.

We are on a diplomatic relations mission. But for the data found from a time capsule at an archaeologist dig, sent into space by a previous species existing before the last blue star phenomenon, we would not have had knowledge of this destructive consequence happening in our system. That is why we have a future inside.

The Web

Chapter 1
Time

Time
The giver
The taker
What is
What is to become
What has been

Don't
Measure yourself by others
But by achievements
By successes and
How you exceed

The Web

The Planet Qua

My first assault on this planet was, no less than, astonishing. I set down where no one would be around to observe or question the assault. When entering the atmosphere of a world we look like a streak in the sky, as though space debris entered and burnt up or like a material shower from a passing meteor, when someone points to the sky and says 'look a shooting star', you don't know, it could be a light streamer. We use the natural effects caused by nature to enter a world's atmosphere.

How many light streamers are on a world at any given time one can only assume? Anyone observing, from a distance, would not suspect it to be anything else, but a shooting star, unless I landed right in front of them.

The plant life will be similar to ours but with a major colour difference. This is a red planet. Although there is colour, differentiating one species from another, the dominant is red. That creates a pigment change in the plant life.

All leaves are various colours of red, yellow, orange, some mauve, and when there is a change of time period of dead leaves and plants they turn a purple decaying shade, deepening in comparison as decay takes over. This colour of decay is also the same for the citizens of Qua. Most of the plant lives are docile which means, they can't move from their rooting area, but there are other types of plant life to fear, and with the difference of evolution colour, they are difficult to differentiate when observed. That's why we use light spectrum contacts they are placed onto our eye lenses and can change the colour spectrum to suit our environment, so differentiating the plant life is more approachable.

That doesn't mean we are safe from attack, as we don't know all the species of this planet, its plant life and parasites. So we are inoculated with an immune booster before jumping and have to be re-injected every half rotation.

Betalains: This is a pigment that creates red and yellow colours in plants this is the dominant pigment found in the plants of this planet. It is the natural evolution stage of our solar system and does not change for 5,000 planet rotations. It is thought that the hostility of this planet, as in the past of my home planet, is caused by the high betalains, and anthocyanins in the plant life of this planet's period of evolutionary time, creating an atmosphere of hostility and highly venomous creatures and plant life. It is the only explanation we have to understand the ferocity of this world's wildlife, vegetation, and inhabitants of inelegance. War and conspiracies are due to jealousy and power and are endemic.

Anthocyanins: this is a pigment that also creates the high brilliance of red in the plant life of Qua, based on the PH. It also causes a spectacular hue in the atmosphere making for beautiful sun spectrums and setting afterglows. Sunsets into darkness are not at all and darkness is caused only by eclipses. But when they do happen the hue is a spectacular red and yellow crest that can, without protection, blind a person instantly.

These pigments dominate the environment and plant life, on Qua. The brilliance of these colours was so overwhelming we had to make special contacts and eyepieces in order to tone down and balance the brightness, so we could distinguish the similarities of plant life, vegetation and animals, or we, the light streamers, would starve or go insane, or be killed quickly by the unknown venomous plants and life forms existing here which was the case when light streamers first began jumping.

Death can still happen in this manner because, we don't know every form, but it is less likely now with these adaptations. And we tend to stay in the more densely populated areas.

Not everyone can be an LS (light streamer) it takes mental awareness and tact; after all, we are streaming into social environments that are new and unpredictable. So being able to read situations and faces and make quick assumptions based on past happenings, and character is important. A bad decision could lead to very extreme circumstances. We go through many test and orientation dialogue before being inserted with the stream source.

After passing the three planetary rotation training periods we are implanted, there are physical changes to consider and punishments to deal with. The physical changes are subtle in context but impactful in punishment. One of the worst is imbibing.

One learns quickly that, past three of anything, there are no limits with some, and others are violently sick, it is then known who fits in what position. Heavy drinkers are given positions of aggressive contact and authority because, on Qua, drinking is a part of the process of negotiation.

Light streaming is referred to as jumping. Light streaming is being sent through space in a beam of light that holds the necessary elements that support living beings. What we are attached to is a grid, one that has engrossed the whole of the planet and the space between so one knows where and when they are. It's not that we have sent the grid out, it's a part of the webs matrix, it's kept in a sphere with two cores that can reproduce any and every nuance, region and land mass of any planet in our system or any other system attached.

By connecting a megalith at each pole of a planet or asteroid we can send light beams anywhere on the surface, then there are interchangeable rings, but these cannot be used until the planet is a part of the Webs matrix. This resource stores energy absorbed by solar rays, it can produce an unlimited supply of power that exceeds the planet's needs.

By manipulating energy, depending on what power is needed at what time, planet to planet interface can bring change slowly or with great speed. This is why there are so many interchangeable rings. We always have interactive citizens on planets that we are integrating with. We are the GODS (to follow the God equation).

Chapter 2
Wild Child

What do you see
 Beyond the mirrored glass
What do you believe
 Watching each world pass
The stories that are told
 As they rip into your veins
Blood staid souls of rock and roll
Come and come again

What do you think
As you look into the mirror
What do you feel
Finding it's not you at all
You like what you see
And the way we play
Bloodstained souls of rock and roll
Come and come again

What do you see
As you look into the glass
What do you know
As the feeling won't pass
You find pleasure
As we sterilize your brain
Bloodstained souls of rock and roll
Come and come again

Love spills into
endless halls
Wild child
As you tear
At the walls
Running wild
Taking life frame by frame
Taking it by another name
Taking the rules
From a different game

There is discontent in the General's quorum, they cannot agree, something is amiss. Although there has been a joining with three of the outer worlds, and work is nearing completion on these planets, a structured agreement to unite all the planetary systems is the only way the grid of *The Web* alignment can work. The largest of the outer worlds has cut off all communication and does not accept the terms that have been presented.

Equality and freedom to all people is not a reality. The dissidence between culture, religion and government is too extreme and they continue to war amongst each other and show no sign of collaboration the ire is strong in the halls of the Empire of Qua.

The outer world, the largest of all the planets in the system, is the most populated, by comparison. The other planets have less land mass and are not as aggressive or are not as evolved. Because of Qua's size and distance from the inner orbiting smaller planets its involvement, in the alignment, is crucial. However, the evolution of its people has been compromised by dysfunction.

There is no single governing body in the province of Zed and Akir, and the multiple tribal factions that separate each other by boundaries and armies, declare to be the first to succeed in history. And will not accept any other law than what has been passed from generation to generation to the present time. Kings and knights are succeeded by admirals and generals. Succession is only realised by war which makes diplomacy impossible.

Time is at a standstill there are no secrets only lies. Spies and deception mask the reality; contradiction and jealousy keep suspicion amongst the councils as they continue to fight within their own tribal societies. The only idea, with Qua, is to reach an agreement with the largest faction, Kranaqus and draw in the remaining tribes with promises of shares to the resources of new technologies and minerals that are constantly the source of all wars.

I am Je-hu and I am telling this story, as I am the last of the original AL Directors.

(Assaulting light) left to tell it. We are an agent of Light Streamers. We have been communicating and acting as diplomats between leaders and Ambassadors as they are in constant flux. Expectant life among the leaders is short as tempers flare very fast leaders become vicious and the killing of anyone in power brings to a halt all discussions that were made during that period.

All talks of unity or peace have to begin again with the newly elected or coup Leaders. And there are many.

This is what frustrates the idea of structure on this planet and what causes continuous war amongst the tribes and provinces. Every large Governing body has power and weapons. Though reluctant to use them, it is only a matter of time before one province acts on its lust for control.

We have light streamers in very few governing clans and tribes. Including Kranaqus where I am stationed as head of the intervention, we have streamers interacting with the leading Klan's. In all it is assumed that there are several hundred of us in this world it is still not enough and that's only on this world alone.

Other than Devi, my home planet, there are four worlds making up a five-planet system. Three have already been integrated with the web. Qua is the last.

Only two of the first three were an easy integration the other two took more planning and a group action done by appealing to the leaders of each of the governing principles Serxho, the third a world of music, will be told at a later time.

There is no other force like us in the known universe but that is also an explanation for another time. The reason for choosing from the citizens is we are a small planet and can only offer a small force plus the citizens have a stronger connection to the issues and there is a greater intelligence surrounding each outcome. The planetary infiltration units are called streamers.

This name is chosen because they stream in and out of social and political society. This gives us a more connected strength to social integration and what they think is going on with the governing powers and issues.

I have just learned of a coup that is set to take place in forty-eight hours. It will be bloody if not stopped, and yet, there is little we can do about it. After assaulting Planet Qua, I found it a hostile planet with tornadoes, hurricanes and monsoons. The most hostility comes from the governing faculty, their people, even if disgruntled; go along with how things are because inside Kranaqus change is not without its price.

Within each lower tribe, there are no elected bodies and they are usually short-lived, as in each family everyone is trained to lead, therefore, the potential to face conspiracies is inevitable.

Jumping is for the most part safe unless disrupted by solar flares, hurricanes or gravitational magnetic anomalies; the assaulting light is always accurate. In the past touchdowns could be off by hundreds of kilometres. This could result in ocean drops which lead to drowning or, in cases of solar flares complete world misses. These happenings are now rare and only occurred when light travel was first discovered.

Since then we are better prepared as we have a constant watch with solar activity and other world weather on all planetary systems. It is much easier than we thought all it takes is the monitoring of each sun to planet location. That means combining the efforts of eighteen land-based observatories. Two focused on each sun and two on each outer world, plus the watch pattern changes of weather on our own planet.

It's set up on a matrix of computer systems that are always in touch with two central locations at each polar cap. As well there are five off-world observatories in the outer region of the web. This gives accurate information at all levels of intelligence, the action of weather and their patterns are all ways watched. Still, there are plans for four more off-world satellite observatories. And this time, as always, my assault was right on.

The crucible of secrets: This is the space capsule found in the archaeologist dig in the desert of my home planet, Devi.

The Architecture of Qua: Glass Structure

The properties for construction used to make walls, interior and exterior.

From my observations Qua has just discovered, in the past fifteen years, a magnetic force that will change their whole planet's structure and evolution of technology as it is seen at this time. We have happened at the best moment in their history. The buildings, though new to this use of structure technique, are magnificent. Non-corrosive steel is used as framing for massive glass panels that create walls, which are held in place by magnetism, the new technology.

The glass is mixed with metals and carbon then tempered, known as annealed glass it gives a stronger and more durable usage. More functional for building, the magnetic metal ends are joined by metal channel. A magnetic force holds the panels in place along with silicon, which acts as an insulator and a buffer against the steel, or concrete framing.

Glass building structures have gone through hundreds of rotations of research to get it to the building strength it is now, and now, with this new discovery, the builders of Qua can make massive glass panes that reach beyond their expectations and have no central joins or seams.

Concrete is the original structure used for framing in glass and is still used on a major scale. The buildings are too rugged and when the seals were compromised the glass faces or walls began to chafe and chip forming cracks and fissures which would cause major shattering compromising the integrity of the glass, sometimes leading to multiple deaths if citizens were standing nearby or inside. That is why steel framing is taking place of concrete.

When there is a magnetic hold, integrating the new technology of steel and plpBusing these large glass panes, it forms a shield that, even when fractured, it is held into place until the magnetic path is disrupted. Before that happens safety measures are taken or replacement to prevent complication.

Magnetism

The new technology discovered, accidentally by an unknown and released by council, fifteen rotations past, has given a different approach to sealing the glass panels to the newly developed frames and forms. Magnetically, these new seals are stronger, less likely to cause cracks or fissures and prevent implosions or explosions off the face, as they are, sometimes, very enormous and actually getting larger with every new construction.

The old seal was against concrete, the frame of the structure would be designed with a concrete form and using a steel channel and I beam, applied with a type of tar, it would seal the glass into place. The tar is created with animal fats from the large ocean dwellers and land beasts. Silicon is a synthetic created to simulate the tar and turned out to be more effective and less compromising on the life forms. But now, with this new technology, steel beams are being used to build towers, and, instead of tar, silicon is being applied to the frame work.

Tar and weather seal is still used as an insulation cushion, but only on smaller structures. Magnetism is the holding source of structure joins. This creates a stronger seal to the buildings frame and a charged force field around the structure that is difficult to penetrate, without being discovered. Exterior securities are more controllable and citizens are less likely to corrupt, or compromise the systems.

Concrete is used only as reinforcement or purely for design. Most architects prefer the steel exposed as a design technique giving a complete glass structure, but will go back to the old use of concrete to offset style, planed as a technique for design. Concrete used in structure formations do not compromise the use of magnetic bonding. The bond is still effective; it just needs to be tweaked with a stronger current.

Stone

Archaeologists, from my planet, have discovered that before the postmodern building structures, the same technique was applied, we have an archive of old building design, materials and how they were formed or created, their uses and application. We don't have to investigate or break materials down to know what is in it.

The stone and concrete work is used as frames for structure. This was the only way to build megastructures and columns that could hold extreme panes of glass.

With the discovery of magnetic bonding against steel beam structure and concrete forms of structure, this changed on Qua, as it did on my world, Devi.

Gothic Structure, Art and Design

The old design was created as art to give a more appealing look. Rather than simple forms of concrete or stone, stone cutters were often brought in to do more intricate designs. And depending on the wealth of the builder and the cost of the design its style would vary in artistic technique.

But as glass took over the building idea stone became less and less as use for structure and more for foundation as metal beams took a more dominant place. Glass was then introduced as a more appealing look and the size of the pane became more paramount in structure magnitude. Also, the appeal of an exaggerated peak known as Goth, or French style is the most common use for topping structures made for business, multiple usages and large area height size.

Citizen dwellings don't take it too extreme for example, government structures, or historical archives and museums. But they can get very artistic and diverse with their building architecture, as well, religious structures.

Structure of Power

Each town is set up like a nest of conspiracy. Each clan has their own structure of ordinances and in it their own agenda. Yet, every clan's itinerary always includes the confiscation of land and position and brings into effect new law and taxation with every coup, or change of reigning faction.

The municipality is set up with governing bodies of administrations; they all follow a strict administration design. The changes are with the faculty who are seated and that happens with every takeover and can happen several times annually. Depending on the strength of the family and alliances formed in the pursuit of power a coup is not always successful, there are many spies and traitors in all alliances and clans. However, it is often in the best interest of business and social function to have administrations change.

Although elections are part of every province a coup disrupts the order of this happening, especially during election years, so a province can go many rotations without an election. Elections are to be held every five rotations, depending on who is in power at the time. Some clans eliminate elections and hold power in a military fascist way. That's when a coup is a certainty, but it can take numerous rotations before anyone clan is strong enough to compromise the power in office.

Strict Administration Structure

Governor:
Secretary:
Vice-president of estates:
(Land tax and disclaimer)
President of the council:
(Citizens' rights and the law)
Trustee:
(All financial exploits)

Every district, municipality and town nest apply to this system of administration; it's the only accepted order with all provinces, states and counties as the law of business and entitlement. All have to be registered. If there is no record of you, you do not exist and can be shot on sight by any who chose to do so, THERE WILL NOT BE ANY LAWLESSNESS! This is a contradiction this whole planet is directed by contrivers and deception, it's amazing how fast records of all who exist can be taken and kept, until all are known.

When death is the ultimate cause to conform, one registers into the system, as the aggressive light is attached to my being, I am, but a ghost.

Chapter 3
As If

You want secrets
To intertwine
You need alibis
Instead of lies
There's not knowing
Then there's showing
What and who
You really are

There's defence
In your every dream
The reasons why
Are in all the meaning
The way you stop
And dare a stare
Telling why
As if you care

You want secrets
And alibis
There's defence
With reasons why
To stop and
Dare a stare
Telling lies
As if you care

As if
You have the gift
As if
You rely on yourself
As if
There is nothing else
As if
It's all been shelved

As if
It was part of the day
As if
Things are still OK
As if
There were more to say
As if, as if
As if

Kranaqus the largest province

Rox (the largest city centred on an Island, but a part of Kranaqus)

The first team of streamers, on the planet Qua, planning the intervention, or deception.

Tumi: Streamer citizen of Qua, tailless, midsize and determined.

Jh-hu: Light Streamer, from the planet Devi, a muscular and agile creature, diplomatic and decisive, a great leader and tactic specialist.

Ohn-ohn: Streamer citizen of Qua as well as the Emperor's head of security. He is of the bread of a citizen with a small tail. Males with tails are of a different hereditary background. Tails on males are always subs.

The Festival

It is a time for rejoicing, a time for celebration and lust. The campaign has been won. Kranaqus has just come from a crusade with Zed. Je-hu is sitting on the crest of a hill, overlooking the city of Rox, observing the rituals of the festivities.

After every campaign, the pick begins, and there is a party, which includes everyone. The prisoners are auctioned off and used for games of torturous sex, games of death, for example, simulations of battles to the death, tortured while being gang-raped and then disembowelled to be prepared for fertilisation of fields and feed for farm animals. Cannibalising the prisoners is also a part of the feast. This is left for the most prominent and the most beautiful.

What is meant by the most beautiful is, if there are women on the battlefield, whores, mistresses, wives, they are separated and kept in a comfortable hold, as a form of deception and, being told that they are special, are prepared for the honour of joining the feast at the end of each day. Of course, as their numbers diminish, they know what is meant by, being prepared. The harvest is also in season at this time so there is much to celebrate.

Only the hierarchy is reserved for the picking honour, generals, admirals, lieutenants and Sergeant, for the festivities. But that is not all that is being celebrated. There is a newly elected Emperor and the people are hoping to see a change in the laws and structure of power. It, the governing body, has been one-sided for too long and, from what has been suggested in speeches given by the newly elected Emperor, change is going to be the topic of discussion.

New members of the committee will be selected. The Emperor has now taken his position and is ready to be ordained. So the festivities have a dual purpose, just two days before, there had been a confrontation with ZED.

KRANAQUS, the strongest governing bureaucracy on the planet, is also the largest populated land region, occupying two-fifth of the planet's continents, which is also the most fertile. Festivals are celebrations of change, winning a campaign, harvest, or honouring the newly elected. And yet, as the festival went on, the committee conspired.

Although there has been an accord with three of the outer worlds and work is complete or, in the final stages of these planets, a structured agreement to the unity of all planetary systems is the only way the Web alignment can work. The largest of the outer worlds has cut off all communication and does not accept the terms that have been presented. Equality and freedom to all people is not a reality. The dissidence between culture, religion and government is too extreme. They continue to war amongst each other and show no sign of compromise the ire is strong in the halls of the Empire.

The Campaign

(Two days earlier)

I, Je-hu, am just an observer. The director of Akir knows the power of Kranaqus and concedes to their laws and bureaucracy. Their war is with Zed. When campaigning, the armies have to consider all the factors.

In this region, there is a tall grass that is carnivorous, on Qua plant life is either docile or carnivorous, as well, fungus and rashes torment the citizens. This grass, known as snake blades, are very lethal, when grown tall, as the victim passes through, the blades reach out to cut into the body of the passer. Touching also injects venom that attacks the nervous system rendering the victim motionless yet still awake while the blades ingest the victims' fluids. There is a simple way through it.

Just cut it down, or burn it. Kranaqus has come up with some elaborate ways to do this. And now with the new technology, the ways of attack have been broadened. Laser light can destroy a whole field in ten and five-tenth's seconds.

As Kranaqus marches through the burnt field of snake's grass to march on Zed.

The Zed army has been waiting behind the field in dugout bunkers and trenches, they have some incredible weaponry, purchased by the Zed army, and after being pirated by the underground forces in Akir, waiting to be launched, they wait.

"All forward" sounded a loud voice over the microphone, as they marched into Zed and the awaiting ambush. Kranaqus has received some inside information and has arranged a different line-up, the captains will remain at the rear of each platoon and the second in charge will lead.

With Zeds knew weaponry, the first five rows of the front lines were evaporated, and the Kranaqus soldiers scattered. The soldier with the laser could then only pick out groups and singles. Because the laser is stationary it can be easily overrun, so it is set in the backfield. Kranaqus will have a difficult time taking it out.

As the soldiers scattered they crossed onto the field, and that's when Zed opened the trench doors, right in the middle of the Kranaqus armies and the generals cried out Berserker, swords and knives along with another new weapon, stolen from Kranaqus called a spectrum. Kranaqus captains were completely surprised by the use of this weapon against them. They had only lost these weapons a few days previous and to see them on the battlefield was a shock.

Because of the mix of warriors the laser could only be shot at random intervals. Though the laser can be set with a beam radius of one metre and evaporate (vaporise) at an extreme distance, it can sweep into much larger groupings. Laser weaponry is rare; it has only just been invented by the weapons specialists in Kranaqus and has been captured by the underground black market in Akir, this is the first time this weapon has been used in battle. It is also being used by Kranaqus but finding it in use against them was startling and confused them on the battlefield with Zed.

But Kranaqus has a few of them and another new weapon called "the Stomper" this was kept highly secret and just made ready for use for this battle. What it does is, after pre-setting the coordinates, it hovers over the selected target and at the pre-set time, of seconds, it sends out a pulsating anti-gravitation force, reversed from the gravitation of the planet's own magnetic force, with an explosive fracture of a bubble that pulls all in the perimeter into its centre and implodes.

Set to the surrounding area not exceeding the set target, so no other ground troops are compromised or taken in. It would make for a short campaign if both sides suffered at the use of this weapon that can eliminate everything on the battlefield with one assault. Pieces of the laser operator, and the five soldiers protecting his position, fell in a ten-foot radius of their position. Too bad Zed only had one laser.

After the laser was taken out Zed retreated, there is no surrendering because all tribes live by, "He who fights and retreats his ground lives to fight another round." This is the rule of all the tribes, clans and armies. So when there are great casualties and losses there are always numerous soldiers ready for the next battle. Now, it is time for the pick.

The outer world, the largest of all the planets in the system, is the most populated of all, by the percentage of land mass. Because of its size and distance from the inner orbiting smaller planets, its involvement in the Webs matrix is crucial. However, the evolution of its people has been slow. There is only one single governing body and that is Kranaqus province, all other provinces have multiple tribal factions that separate each other by boundaries and armies.

Each declares to be the first to succeed in history and will not accept any other law than what has been passed from generation to generation to the present day. Kings and knights are succeeded by admirals and generals, admirals and generals succeeded by barbarians and uncivilised. Succession is only realised by war which makes diplomacy impossible. Time is at a standstill there are no secrets only lies.

Spies and sorcery mask the reality; contradiction and jealousy keep suspicion amongst the councils as they continue to fight within their own. The only idea is to reach an agreement with the one largest empire and draw in the remaining tribes with promises of shares to the resources that are constantly the source of all wars.

I am just five miles outside of my destination; this is done to keep a low profile on how light streamers are projected from one world to another. The few streamers I have in my unit are already assembled and it will take me at least one hour to walk the distance to their location. They are just outside the city of Rox.

Rox is located on an Island, in the land of Kranaqus. My crew knows who the target is and who is going to pull off the assassination but when and where are the questions that have yet to be answered.

As I approach the cave, where we hold up and plan, I am greeted by Tumi.

"Hey."

"Hey to you."

"Je-hu we've been waiting here for hours," Tumi, the captain of the streamers, said impatiently.

"Well, it's better than spending time digging in the muddy fields, isn't it? And to be honest I was observing the battle at the border of Zed."

"Oh, you don't have to tell us how it went we can probably guess. We have an idea where the coup is going to come from, and what positions we should be taking in order to intervene."

"Ya, I've put myself right in the centre of the ambassadors' assembly that way I can be right in the middle of the confrontation, I'm the head bodyguard and can act on any suspicious characters in the crowd," said Ohn-ohn, the systems director of streamers.

"How long have you been observing the Melissa?" asked Je-hu.

"A few days, though, they've been very slick keeping a low profile, something they did was out of the ordinary and didn't fit the norm." Ohn-ohn fumbled with his belt. He was looking for a map hidden in his buckle. It was crudely drawn but effective.

Ohn-ohn continued, "This is a total layout of weapons, guard positions and points of attack. The only thing missing is, at what time. But that will be answered as the day progresses with the festivities it will be known when the Emperor plans his entrance to join the games. Festivals are always held after a campaign and goes on for days.

"No one knows when the Emperor will join the festivities but it is always announced and his entrance is always from the same unguarded area."

At that moment, Je-hu interjected, "But we will be waiting, we cannot let this happen. Too many times progress has been quashed due to overthrown governments and tribal wars. This time we have an inside man working with us. Ohn-ohn is the right hand, the Lieutenant of the guards and can give an inside account of what is happening around the Emperor and the Empire."

Ohn-ohn went on to say, "The festivities usually start with a parade of the armies, right off the battlefield, progressing into large dining halls where the people of the country gather to celebrate the success of the campaign. Then at some point, the Emperor addresses the quorum to enlighten the people of the future of the Empire. It happens just before the final course of the feast."

As Je-hu approached the others he noticed that they were looking at what was laid out on the floor. A game, on the board, was written the word Campaigne, this is the most important thing they will learn from my world and on into their own future. Especially the way they are so prone to war on each other, we are here, not to change them but to only grab two-acre plots to build the necessary monoliths for the enhancement.

The work has already begun on the polar caps and several offshore areas, but there have to be land-based towers strategically placed around the continents and Islands to make it effective on a planetary level and interaction with the orbiting planets. This matrix is to be duplicated on every planetary system and this world is the last.

The team were all standing around staring at the game while Je-hu began setting up.

"This," Je-hu began, "Is the game Campaigne, a game of strategies that will help us in this quest of infiltration and occupation. We need plots of two acres and that means encountering the ruling factions. We don't know, until we infiltrate the largest kingdom, Kranaqus what or whom we are to deal with. This first infiltration is the most important It will give overall freedom to finding the best positions on the globe and in each specific province, state and county."

"But first the game."

"Campaigne has a story that must be told while learning, to understand why it has the strategies it has, to adapt it into battle because; as we play so shall we fight, first, how to set it up.

The Empress sits on the furthest diamond, this is home base or the kingdom, then in front of her sits the Emperor, between the Empress and Emperor (Dragon), sit the pyramids, the Archers sit to the left and right of the Emperor (Dragon) and right in front of the Emperor (Dragon) sit the chariots. Then seven minions as front pieces, one on each side of the board beside the Archer and five across the front."

As Je-hu showed them, he began the story of its history and the use of each piece.

"Now, the story begins, this is a legend that has been passed to all who learn Campaigne. It is a story of betrayal and deceit and it is based on fact. In our history we have a very shady past; our Emperors have taken liberties where none should have been expected. During times of the Great War, when things are uncertain, to get knowledge of tactics, future campaigns, strategies, certain sacrifices are made. And it is in this action that wars are lost and won. It is known as the Mask.

"The Emperor, for strategic purposes, would use the women and wives of the soldiers as spies or traitors, to obtain knowledge of the opposition. Where they are camped, what they may be planning, how many in each company, and plan of attack. Anything that could give an edge to winning the campaign and that is what we are going to work with. The Mask is the best strategy. And is the most successful because it is the most underhanded and unexpected deception."

"So, let me tell you the story," Je-hu sat and crossed his legs.

"After decades of rotations the war's end was still not in the foreseeable future, so the Emperor, in all his great wisdom, came up with a plan. He sends for all the brides and mistresses of each soldier to do an inspection for the most beautiful, the most cunning, wicked and sly. The selection is in teams of seven, they are to report to a team leader, usually one of the ranking soldiers and a liaison, with one of the wives.

"That way there will be little room for treachery. In other words, to betray the empire and lose the edge that was needed; which is what this action was directed to do. Well, this plan of attack worked for many centuries and still does, in the right circumstances, but only once was it taken to an extreme by one of our Emperors, letting it get out of control, taking it to the ultimate betrayal. Emperor, Ayyaz, did not know how to maintain loyalty and fell to the most tactless errors in battle, he sent his queen out to act as a traitor.

"He didn't know that she was unhappy. Bored with the way of life he had provided and needing something more than the dealings of tactlessness and uncouth behaviour. Ayyaz was accustomed to giving, as well, having to share the estate with the other spouses.

When she volunteered he, the Emperor, was pleased that she took an interest in the outcome of this campaign, which was a bloody one, and needed a special inside infiltration tactic, to use the Empress was an excellent opportunity to take advantage of, so she was trained. Mistake number one; relying on someone that is looking for adventure, not a resolution, which puts the whole outcome in jeopardy."

Je-hu then turned to the game and began to explain, "Everything stops at the centreboard and can only cross one half of the diamond at a time, once crossed they can resume their usual moves around the second half of the board. Except for the minions, they move one diamond at a time. The objective is to put one of the opposing pieces at the opposite end of the board that determines the winner of the game."

Je-hu began to set up again and explain where each of the pieces sits.

The Dragon: It sits on the end of the board holding the off on involvement until the Empress switches places. Then he has a full range of the board, moving in any direction.

The Empress: It sits in front of the dragon and can only move one diamond at a time.

The Minions: They move two diamonds anywhere on their side of the board but once they cross the centreboard, they only move one diamond at a time. They can only kill on opposing colours and forward, not backward.

Once across the centreboard, they cannot return.

The Pyramids: They stand between the Empress and the dragons, black diamond on the red, white diamond on the black, they can move horizontal and vertical.

The Archers: They stand one on white and one on black, together on the left of the Emperor and can only travel and kill on their own colour.

On both sides of the board, one half of the diamond only at the centreboard.

The Chariots: They stand on the right of the Emperor and have an abstract as an L move and must always move and kill on the opposite colour. With their moving difference, they are the only pieces that can use their move to cross as long as it stays on the first half of the diamond at the centreboard, when crossing.

The game is based on this story, which is also a Love story. The game is also based on treachery and the element of treason. The King sends his Empress to liaise with the prince of the opposition to establish inside knowledge with future battle plans. She is sent with information vital to the outcome of the next campaign and makes herself available.

She hints so subtly with a suggestive taunt and a kiss, to have an affair with the emissary, the ultimate goal, without being pulled into the emotion. The Empress has a very wicked mind, she, upon seeing the valiant majestic wit of the prince, began her deceit. To abdicate the issues on both sides and miss inform on both sides this war can keep going forever. Their armies are equally matched and it is in both sides best interest to win.

At that moment, Tumi was conversing with one of his spies with news about the fair. As the main course was finishing something unusual happened. The Emperor's entrance was changed, there was no announcement. The dessert is served with no introduction it seems the Emperor is not going to even address the house.

"Je-hu, we have a problem" Tumi is on cam, recorder link; our technology is more advanced than anything on this planet. And we have a stronger link to everything in range with the frequency.

"What's up?"

"Ohn-ohn's found the Emperor, and he's dead," said Tumi.

"What can you make of it?"

"He said, it's red ire; there are five dead by his body and more around the table. He put up a good fight but it looks like he was swarmed. By the bites on his body it looks like tens of thousands," said Tumi.

"Ohn-ohn checked the source and thinks they were encased in the moulds of assorted cheeses. This has been planned for months. They were obviously bred inside the cheese while it was being cured. That's the only way they could have gotten inside.

They must have been put in while in their cocoons, mummified, waiting to be cut into by the unsuspecting. Red Ire, when encased in or trapped by moulds or fungi, they are dormant until released by a wandering animal or the curious soul looking for food, quite the surprise for the poor sucker doing the preparations."

Tumi went on to say, "And in this situation, it appears as though the Emperor insisted on making the first cut into it, as it is known that the Emperors elected are connoisseurs of all cheeses and…"

"And did so, so it seems, as only the ones closest to the target were attacked," Ohn-ohn said, as he observed the scene.

"So, how many are dead?" Je-hu asked.

"Two chiefs, three cooks and the Emperor, several servers, there may be more outside. If we search the grounds we may find there are more in the mix." Tumi emphasised.

"Oh, well that makes for quite the replacement costs! As well."

"How do we approach this from an investigation standpoint?" Tumi asked.

"We go to the cheese manufacturer and start with the maker of this particular batch," Je-hu suggested.

"That should get a good start to finding who's responsible and give us an idea of how deep this conspiracy goes. Or at least a lead, to put us on the right trail of this suspicious event." directed Ohn-ohn "I'll get back to Tumi with whatever is discovered in the next 48/72 hours. We, Tumi and I, will then get back to you with what is discovered."

Je-hu; the light streamer, an agent from the central world, Devi, is a tall reptilian-like creature. Walking on two legs he also has the power of the light, a matrix of the web tied to a central force on his home planet.

Tumi; the leader of the streamers, on Qua, in Je-hu's quorum, a muscular well-kempt warrior who, from a different evolution of planetary sequence, also a two-legged walking creature with the reptilian likeness, with a small stub for a tail.

Ohn-ohn; the second in command in the quorum of streamers, as well, until the assassination of the Emperor, first guard to the Emperor. He like Tumi, who is a two-legged walker, but these creatures have no tails. Only the females have tails.

This world's delicacy is cheese, if there is food, cheese is served with it, at breakfast it is cheese if nothing else. Cheese of life is the cheers of life and it is the cheers of life that give the world its character. In this world, cheese is their character.

"Wow, this changes everything."

Je-hu went on to say, "I think we are in for a long ride, from what I have observed, there is something going on in the kitchens, as well, we need to investigate."

Je-hu got up and walked around the room while continuing to observe his team. "It seems, from what I've been observing, that the kitchen is a part of the conspiracy If not the whole action depends on the chefs and cooks to do their part to make everything happen. Who does the responsibility fall on to after the death of the Emperor?"

"The council," answered Tumi.

"Also, we have to find a suitor, to sit as Emperor who does not like or cannot eat cheese," Je-hu suggested.

"Well," Tumi responded, "that is a difficult one, the only way we can consider that is to find a rarity, the person has to be elected and have a rare syndrome. An allergy to cheese and cannot eat it due to an extreme reaction being, rashes and symptoms that can result in death."

He went on to say, "We will have to dig deep into the elected body and see who we come up with and direct his or her political platform to becoming Emperor."

"Tumi," Je-hu said, "Find the best candidate for that task, we have only time to count on and if he or she is young it will take more than just direction but real leadership. So go over all who are elected into office including rural, county and sub-municipal. Find someone to fill that position."

As they set about their strategies, looking for the conspirators and to find a rare syndrome in the next Emperor in order to direct the candidate into the Emperor's seat. Also, the need to put together a team of spies to be interjected into the estate staff and find what the typical practices of the kitchen are after an Emperor is elected. Teaching a bunch of barbarians campaigned and planning the next course of action, there will be another battle and Je-hu has to find out when and where. All this before the next election in two years.

Meanwhile, the committee can direct their conspiracies, of which there will be many, at the people they govern, as they try to keep the peace. Not easy when you're the governing council and no one trusts what you do. And for good reason, their government is the power that is ripping the people apart. Through taxation, immigration, food, supplies, product, basically anything that moves or can be moved, sold or used for any purpose. Forty-five per cent of all wages and transport goes to tax.

We are the resistors, and we will overcome the conspiracy of the governing council, with strategies and cunning. It will take several teams to infiltrate and several candidates. One for each political ridding, there are three governing oppositions that seem to always be fighting for position and, it seems, that no matter which of the parties that find themselves on the Emperor's seat the committee is always the victor.

It's about the wars, business and land, slaves and whores, people to bring home for the wife and children, toys if you will, as they are only around until the next campaign. Then everyone fights, women, men, boys, girls and nobody brought in from the last campaign comes home. That's when the committee has the most fun when nobody lives and the only way to survive is to stop at nothing, to go berserk until you get to the other side of the battle's end.

Then, what lay waiting is the prize, the commander, killed in battle or fleeing the loss, would leave all his valuables to the victor. In the past when going into battle all who are present were to be used for pleasure and as pawns during the next campaign. This is known as 'The Emperor's Cross' and is derived from darker times. Devi has evolved from that history but Je-hu carries the journals, from that period with him.

Emperors Cross has a duality, the Queen can also exchange positions with the Emperor and is ready to play (do battle). She can then roam anywhere on the board, at any time during the game she can go renegade, crossing to the opposing army, or chose to stay on the side of her Emperor. Only the Queen can do this.

All pieces cannot cross the centreboard until the dice roll, the half diamond (centreboard) is the cross over. Dice are used for the centreboard crossing, by rolling a one or a five to resume your moving ability, and then the chosen piece can cross.

Emperors Cross: the position of Empress and Dragon are exchanged, leaving the Empress to move at will. She also stops at the centreboard throws the dice and moves, only one half of the diamond, before continuing with her freedom and treachery. If she is captured she can be used as a renegade only if she is captured by pyramids. She can be killed by any piece.

Definition, Red Ire: crab-like spiders, as venomous as the black widows of earth, but with a tainted difference when emerging from their cocoons, as babies, they are very aggressive, or when grouped together they become very aggressive and attack anything.

Chapter 4
One to Find
Child's Play

This way and that
 As a matter of fact
It's a game
 Young kids play
So they say
 Tag your it
But it's
 Not in the script
It's what the
 Headstone might say

In teams if you dare
 Terrors always there
Don't let your mind
 Run askew
So many yet so few
 And you wonder
Where to run to
 Things aren't always
What it seems none

It's not what you think
 Or what you might believe
And today is gone again
 Looking is not seeing
Or what the line is reading
 It's all how it's planed

Hidden in full view
 And you wonder where
To run to
 Still playing in the rain
So many yet so few
 As a matter of fact
It's what the headstone
 Might say
It's all child's play

It's all child's play to me
 It's what's real or fantasy
It's what will or won't be seen

Hi

It's just child's play

The elected, in all there are about 405 elected governing offices over all of the Provinces, one chieftain, three representatives and five elected council members, in each county. There are forty-five counties and the head of all the elected are the remaining five to make a total of 405. These top five, The Committee, are voted in by the elected body of chieftains.

Once seated, they are lifetime members that control the province as the Emperor's council. They make the laws, the tax legislation guidelines and can only be vetoed by the Emperor, if he/she should live long enough to serve, the only considerations to becoming a committee member are to be holding a seat in any riding and hold a transcript of the proprietor.

Je-hu stood in front of Tumi and Ohn-ohn, "We are in a deep chasm. This person needed to take the Emperor's seat will be difficult. He needs to have a stigma to cheese.

Tumi sat back, "*Who can I put into this research*?" He thought, "*There are so few people with that kind of stigma there is only one way to discovery and that is at the historical archives.*"

As he pondered the thought of this, at that moment Ohn-ohn walked in.

"Well, we can let that take its time to resolve," he said.

Tumi replied, "What?"

"The kitchen," said Ohn-ohn. "I have sent five streamers to go in and work it as spies. We have two as janitors, one as security and two working with the cooks. All we need is someone for them to report to."

"Oh, yes. Give me the list of names, and I will have someone assigned to it. We have another matter to attend to that is much more pressing," Tumi remarked.

And, while looking at Ohn-ohn, realised at that moment that the person he's been thinking about is standing right in front of him. Ohn-ohn. He's perfect; he has influence and is known and has charisma.

"I have a very important assignment for you, it involves everything you are and have been doing; therefore, you will be right at home with this. You should be able to find who we're looking for and easily find him or her, because you are already known in the political forum, they will trust you and be quick to impress," Tumi exclaimed.

"It sounds intriguing, what is it?" asked Ohn-ohn.

"We need an infiltrator to the Emperor's seat, someone who is not happy with the way the province is being directed, who is easily influenced and influential as well quickly oriented to be in with this deception and maintain a strong value to change to lead the campaign in the next election. The ideal candidate must not betray our intentions and give no concern to the others in power, such as the Quorum.

"They cannot be suspect, show any deviance of principle and demonstrate only loyalty to them. This person must have influence and be trusted. We arc in the midst of an internal conspiracy and it's important that we know what it is and who is at the source," said Tumi.

"Also, everyone you find must have a rare disorder to cheese. Being that they are already elected they know how to hide this indifference and can overcome its prejudice."

"Well, that sounds a lot harder than it is. I have access to all the records of the elected and their constituency. Although this is a rare syndrome, it just might be the conundrum that can bring this project to be realised. It's not as rare as one might think, but, to find someone in the elected body? That's what makes the challenge intriguing and yet suspenseful," Ohn-ohn retorted.

"OK, then we agreed; you'll pull your resources together and get back to me with what you've found," Tumi glanced at the door. "What will you need?"

Tumi continued, "We have several streamers at your disposal and can be there for what you put together." Tumi and Ohn-ohn then showed tribute.

Ohn-ohn sat to mull over the next steps. "I'll get back to you about that but first I have to go into the files and find the list of the newly formed elected, go through their medical histories and find the right candidate. It's going to take some time, and it isn't easy. Most of the records are sealed and I'm going to need help with that," said Ohn-ohn.

Tumi left to go find Je-hu to inform him of the success of this meeting and find a replacement for the handling of the kitchen operatives.

Ohn-ohn knew that all the records he needed are in the historical archives building, but, there are procedures before getting into the files of medical histories. The only way it can be done is through the Quorum (committee). That will create suspicion and bring on many questions so Ohn-ohn has to find another way and that proposes a problem.

Discretion is the key so it will have to be done after hours when offices are closed. It will take a great deal of planning and at least two streamers to execute this action. The building is heavily guarded and can't be accessed without compromising the security systems that he himself recently directed.

There is a particular reason why there is so much put into security, in the medical building. When being elected to a position or seat it would compromise your character if it were known that you have a disorder or disability not seen by the naked eye, if you have had surgery or issues that will conflict with the longevity, and life of your seat, or reasons to give the opposition any edge to win over you. It is imperative that anything medical is left locked to keep elections equal.

Anyone can campaign but only the strategists seem to be able to hold a seat. They are the ones that seem to be the most persuasive, by design, it isn't by chance.

In the past, here have been lower classes, uneducated, who try to run in campaign's but have failed, due to the exposure of records of medical history, education and ideology. Voting citizens do not like to know that the elected have anything physical to compromise their representation, while in office, as it puts a strain on all business and progress. So the Historical and Medical Archives building was made to impede any knowledge of candidates campaigning which would compromise their right to privacy and their being elected.

So, twenty-five rotations ago it was passed that all records be guarded as to not bring in any issues of health, or impropriety is introduced at the time of campaigning, Then, to safeguard the citizens' privacy, an archives building was founded to hold all records.

The building has the most sophisticated electronics available and the strongest walls and doors to keep breaking into the impossible. Bombs, mechanical or any other means of destruction will not fracture the building. The manpower is also to the maximum, guards on every floor and at every door twenty-four hours a day. It is not without reason, this building is assaulted at least once every three to six times during an orbiting rotation.

The people who are interested in the records are the most notorious and would only have to present the public with a few of these files to set up many council members for blackmail, kidnapping or hostage-taking. But Ohn-ohn has an edge, himself. He has been in that building many times and knows the outline of it, how it's set up for guarding, and was there when the new alarm systems were set in place. He knows how they work and what they do. After all, he was the commanding guard to the Emperor, who is now dead, so of course.

Ohn-ohn is left without a position and the leadership falls to the Committee of five again.

That is a very suspicious thing, as soon as there is a conflict with the Emperor, he dies, and they, the committee, are suddenly taking over the direction of Kranaqus. And this time, it happened before the Emperor could take his seat before he could address the people, and therefore, the plan is afoot.

There are secrets in these walls, entrances that only Ohn-ohn knows of, tunnels, long since forgotten because the inner battles of the political forums are over and have been for decades. They are known by the elected committee, but the threat of inner feuding is past so these escape routes haven't been needed and have been lying dormant and forgotten by most and ignored by the committee. Waiting, waiting for this moment to intervene, uncompromising, uninhibited, and there are several exterior exits (entrances). These tunnels are not a part of any whiteouts, prints of the building plans, and yet they are there.

To find the exits from the outside is complication and will be difficult to find. But they are there, and with a little digging, they will be located. With Ohn-ohn and two other streamers looking, though it will take time, there should be no problems as they are out of the public's view and at least a mile away from the records facility.

Ohn-ohn has been in one of them, from the inside, and knows the direction of the exit so estimating where it comes out is still a guess, but it can be calculated to an almost exact location. Still there will be some searching, though we have only three it will take hours before it is realised and can be entered. And, as it has been said, we only need one route.

"OK, I know by the whiteouts where the corridors are. I have been in them and know the walls," said Ohn-ohn.

Nayrr was observing the whiteouts (blueprints) on the table.

Ohn-ohn went on to say, "We need the layout so I can get a good idea of the direction we have to go."

Nayrr, the first recruit, is an electronic brain and can troubleshoot anything.

Once when we were in a heavily guarded ammo dump our position was compromised by a small creature, we didn't even know what it was. Alarms started sounding all around us except in the building we were in. It was amazing, but before we entered, Nayrr set a fused trap in the main circuitry and, if anyone or thing created a motion problem the only alarms that would activate were the central housing units.

These places are where the staff is housed and it would wake everyone up creating major confusion and it'd be hard to detect who was in the yard. When alarms go off everyone is evacuated and searched, no matter the time. We had an easy escape nonetheless, and with all, we went in for as well.

"I need to know where the mains are," said Nayrr.

"That's the tricky part," Ohn-ohn replied. "They're there in the shed and we are going to be underground so as we're about to enter the building, here, there will be no time or way to disable the systems from this point so it all has to be done from the inside."

"Oh!"

"The wiring can only be accessed once inside the building and that's when it gets tricky. The walls and ceilings are the only areas not sensitised but I have an idea around that, yet, we still need the alarms deactivated because we have to walk around, there is no escaping that, we have to act fast once inside and once we have what we need." Ohn-ohn said, "We still have to make our escape."

"Well, that's the complication, isn't it?" Nayrr replied.

"So the first thing we need to do is get equipped. Naveen, you're in charge of gathering the materials for scaling the walls and ceilings. Nayrr, you know what you need, study the whiteouts and gather your tools be as light as possible, so, the less the better."

Naveen, the second recruit, her expertise is mountain scaling and medicine. She will know exactly what we're looking for and know, by observation, where we need to be. Everything is marked and labelled so she can take us right to the proper filing area without complication or wasting time. Even though we have five days there are a lot of cabinets to go through and we need an expert.

"We meet back here in a week, ready. It's not far off so no screwing around," said Ohn-ohn. "Myself, I will locate the entrance and get it prepared. It will take some scouting and digging once located. We have our work cut out; let's move."

Having two white-outs was the right thing to do Nayrr needs to study what he is involved with and Ohn-ohn needs to scale out where the entrance is. As they depart to their layers a salute, the gesture of alliance, is made.

At his place, Ohn-ohn unfolds the print and starts to scale the tunnel. Although he shone a light beam down the passage there was no way to tell if it had deviated or was just a straight corridor. So it is mainly guesswork all he knows is the exits were set a mile from the building so as to breach the medical grounds and be outside the perimeter.

He can find the wall with the door, inside the building, but the rest is to question so he got an area map to better find the most likely placement hidden and unsuspecting. As he contemplated over the map a while he began to notice, around the perimeter of the medical fencing there are specific planted gardens almost as though they were a part of a pattern, a shape, a sequence of placement. It isn't obvious but if you stare long enough it starts to appear.

The shape is something known and not common which makes it very hard to recognise. He stared longer at the white-outs rest of the day and into the late hour, as the early day began to break he started feeling punchy and went to bed.

Naveen knew exactly where she was heading, her event room, where she prepares for tournaments and bouts, "*where to begin*." She thought.

"*Simple and light, stable and... Yes*."

Still thinking, "*I have an idea, hmm, tricams-six, climbing slippers, three hundred wire nuts, carabineers-six, oh I can't forget about the helitrak harnesses I'll grab the petzl and fatigues. That's it then, I think, for the important stuff now it's just the incidentals. Gloves, I have a stash somewhere in this place, ah Castelli's, a day pack for each of us. Last, rope mini spools but they only come in fifty-feet length six will be needed.*

"*Now, since we are going to be gone for five days we need food, what is light and non-perishable? Granola bars, fruits all prepared water. I have to do some shopping.*"

Nayrr sits on the porch with the white-outs, he requires two. One, the layout of the electrical installations of the security systems and the floor plans. Matching each floor is going to take time and then distinguishing the wires from each other at least there's a colour code, Two, the layout of floor plans to the building.

He scans both, then gets the table to get a closer look at the wires follow them from the shed here to this wall, OK, colours red, yellow, black, blue, green, mark each one and where they lead, cool. They're separated into bundles of four and four separate entrances yes that makes it easier to distinguish and eliminate. Making the list is next, each party gets a copy. It needs to be done together.

"*So, it starts here the walls are ten feet and the cavity is in each corner, the floor grid comes in on the lower corner for the floor systems and lower beams, top two corners will be the videos and the other corner will be the top beams. Now then, the plan will be me in the top corners and Naveen and Ohn-ohn in each of the floor clusters. Tools, three types of pliers and tape two kinds, there are boxes on each outlet two sets of bits and electric screwdrivers. It's easier to find the right wires from inside the box than combing through the casing. They will be specifically marked so we can find them right from the source.*"

Nayrr continues thinking to himself, "*Paper, pen and the layout cameras and upper beams are mine so I'll start with their systems, ground is always green for ministry buildings and medical hospitals. Floor grid blue, it's known that whatever colour the beams the wire is the same, floor grids are always blue, area beams, red (ceiling lights) or orange (wall displays) the only way it could get complicated is if it has the two colours on the same system and no separation, then differentiating will be hard.*"

But Nayrr is optimistic. "*We should have no problems. The video comes with their 'on' wiring and is always black. There it is, Naveen and Ohn-ohn have the blue and orange, I have the black and red. Anything else doesn't apply. There can only be what there is because it was installed after the building was already ten years old distinguishing old from new will be easy, the security s only three years old, no problem. Now to put the kits together, three, we'll be working on our own so we need to all be carrying. I hope Naveen doesn't go overboard with equipment,*" Nayrr thought to himself.

Ohn-ohn sat down just as there was a knock at the door, "Je-hu, what's up?" asked Ohn-ohn.

"Just on my way to meet with the kitchen team to put them in order; Have you come up with anything yet, a plan or……what?"

"This is what we've worked out so far, Naveen is in charge of the climbing equipment and Nayrr is on the electrical. They're working on the plan now I'm just getting ready to go over where to be looking, for our point of entry, we should be ready to go in next week if all goes as planned," said Ohn-ohn.

"Oh? During the week of honour," Je-hu replied.

"Yes, everything is shut tighter than a ship's hull." Ohn-ohn gestured. "It will be quiet and the only thing to worry about is the alarms and maybe three or four guards. Plus if it takes longer to locate the records we have the time."

"Good thinking, the faster the better and we need as much time, to prepare for the election campaign, as possible. Coaching and embellishing the speeches, we have two years but we need to know who. I'll let you get started I've got some planning to do myself so we'll talk later. See ya," Je-hu said.

Ohn-ohn went to the layouts and began looking them over. He knows approximately where the entrance is that's the starting point, it takes a thirty-degree angle from the wall and heads straight out into the forest one mile from the building, in front of the fencing at least one hundred yards from it. Circling the area to search and making a point of two particular bush sights specifically, hoping that there won't be anything else after it is found, we only need one entrance, tomorrow I'll make my first search.

The next day he gets up early and prepares a light snack, while eating there's a knock at the door. Walking over and opening it he's surprised by the figure before him. It's Naveen.

"Hi," Ohn-ohn said.

"Hi," Naveen said sheepishly.

"You're not finished putting the gear together already, are you?" Ohn-ohn asked.

"No, I'm just bringing what I have so I don't have too much to bring at once. Can you help me bring them in, please?" she asked.

"Sure," he replied.

As we were getting the packs of, what I thought was only going to be equipment, Naveen, opens the door of her transport and reaches in to pull out, boxes of stuff, food, junk food? Boxes?

So I softly asked, "What's this?"

"Ooooooh, it's five days, isn't it," she sighed plus the planning and," she stops and gazes into Ohn-ohn's eyes and licks her lips. As Ohn-ohn is carrying two of the boxes, it looked like five or six of them were still left in the transport, plus the equipment bags, and what's inside of them?

Going up the stairs, as he looked over his left shoulder she winks and bends to pick up one box, ONE box! I think my plans are changing, this is going to be all day.

"This is it then?" he asked.

"No, there are still a few items of equipment to be gotten."

Well, the equipment bags look reasonable, I'm just wondering about all this other stuff. Just then, he didn't know if he imagined it or if he invited it. Naveen brushed her breasts against his face while he was placing the last box on the floor.

Was it innocent? Or… he stood up and faced her and began to notice what she's warring, very little, but strangely it's what she showed up in. A trench coat, but it wasn't until she took off her trench coat that he started to become interested.

He stared back and started to remove the strap from around her shoulder, slipping it down her arm. He leaned in to whisper, “I want to taste you and bit your neck.”

She slapped him and stood back as her filmy top silkily slipped over her head. She stood there, in all her splendour, exposed to him and answered the gesture with a hard backhand; fortunately, he was expecting it and moved. With surprising swiftness, she wrapped her tail around his throat and pulled him into her saying “You knew and still waited this long” as she pressed her torso tighter, her breasts full and warm, firm and healthy, ready for him.

My lips kiss them and he began to lick and suck, like a little boy on his mother at feeding time. She moans and sighs pushing him to his knees and bites her thighs as he held her arms around her back. He massaged her sweetness, caressing her cheeks, his tongue enters her between the lips of her button and into her essence, tasting her sweetness, and again, he bites her thighs and cheeks. She moans and thrusts her hips against his face and moans louder as his fingers enter her button feeling the moistness…

The next morning.

“So,” Ohn-ohn started, “What’s all of this?” he questioned.

“Well, five days is a long time to go without anything so I brought some food for us, that’s all,” she shrugged.

“How are we going to carry all of this?” he suggested.

“You think it a little much?”

“Just a little, I think we need to tone it down to one handbag easy carrying snacks, don’t you agree.”

Naveen nodded yes.

Chapter 5
The Kitchen

All of the poems that begin each chapter are Je-hu's writing and there will be more, it's all thoughts, of what is going through his mind at the time of their conception. His writing is poetry or, in his mind, unfinished songs, the trials, regrets, of relationships in question, past loves, all the possibilities that were and are probable.

I Haven't Left

The walls are
Weeping in colour
Whispering on suspended leaves
Alibies of a
Black or white lover
Wondering where you
Were abound
And you found,

There
And nowhere
It's all about the same
Here and
Everywhere
It's the part
I have to play
Anyway

I haven't left
Yet I'm
So far away
Nothing is
What it seems
Escaping
The thought of you

The walls are
Weeping in colour
About the same here
About the same
Inspired by a
Black or white lover
Unwritten alibies
Silent cries
Mistaken

I haven't left yet

Tumi (outside contact)

Sora, a sleek and alluring citizen whom others open up to and offer information and gossip about almost anything, is genuinely a listener with little to offer, other than opinion or criticism, which tends to keep the information, from the intended subordinate (kitchen help and spy team leader).

Nehan, a shy yet curious citizen, who seems unobtrusive, yet can seemingly get into the right association (kitchen help).

Aa-z, Raju (janitors), Aa-z is a tall lanky undefined citizen who is easily overlooked and unobserved. Raju, a bigger character round in body type, but also less likely to play such a role and would be overlooked. Together they can gather great intelligence.

Yasir (security) is a tall muscular citizen well suited as a security placement in this menagerie of spies.

After leaving Ohn-ohn's apartment he begins walking to their lair to find out who Ohn-ohn has found for him. It's quite a distance outside the city and it takes an hour to walk it. Entering he sees four streamers, as they stand to attention, saluting he introduces himself.

"My name is Je-hu and I would like each one of you to introduce yourselves as though you've just met, we're not all here and who are we waiting for."

Just then a female flies into the room and slams the open door, to close it behind her. She is blond, petite but tall five foot eight inches, big green eyes and still wearing her work clothes, not someone you would think to be a baker and not someone who would be suspect as a spy or traitor.

"Sorry, I'm late, but I was kept longer at work and had to run the whole way so as not to keep you wondering."

"Well, then," said Je-hu, "you can begin the introduction part by telling us your name."

"I am Sora, I work as a baker and the reason I'm late is that we were behind with clean up so I stayed longer to help."

"Good, then we can rely on you to do the same at your new position in the Emperor's kitchen? Yes" asked Je-hu.

"Yes," Sora said. "I know how important this is, when being briefed by Ohn-ohn, so you can expect my full cooperation."

"Excellent and it is all right to be late suspicion is the last thing we need, that goes for everyone here. If you are required at any moment to stay longer at your jobs you stay. Even if there is a scheduled meeting, you never know what might be overheard, it could be important; rescheduling is much better than not being in the know of any information that might be passed."

Je-hu then asked, "So what is your position in the kitchen?"

"I make the bread and desserts, which include the serving of the cheeses before, during and after the meal; I receive the entire product that relates to the making of everything in that department. Most of what we use is stored in the pantry or cooler and the freezer is usually not an area that we keep anything in unless it is held overnight or ice cream." Sora decided to stop there feeling that enough was said.

"The cheeses, hmmm, excellent you have a very important position, it is imperative that you get as much knowledge about all deliveries. Where they come from, who makes them and, most importantly, how they are made?"

"Next, we have." As Je-hu points to the far wall, he was leaning against the wall and smoking, butting the gaf out on the counter, he said, "Nehan!"

He is a short, big buffalo of a man. His size shows his love of food and the care he would take in its preparation and portions, his shiftiness crates suspicion but also adds an element of questionable loyalty. Is he here with us or to act as a double agent, this is Je-hu's suspicion and his edge.

"What is your position?" Je-hu asked.

"Sues Chef, I make sure all the menus are prepared two weeks before anyone knows what is being served," he said. "That way if anything is needed it can be ordered with plenty of time so there are no disappointments or confusion of ingredient."

"Right on, two key positions, this is better than I was expecting. Ohn-ohn didn't tell me any of your positions, and I was worried that it was because there were no major rolls, so I guessed he wanted me to learn about them from all of you," Je-hu exclaimed.

"Tell me about the kitchen and the position of the sous chef, Nehan."

"It's unlike any I've ever seen, there are two works over flames, they call them stationary woks, most of the kitchens I've been in have woks that can be used by tossing and mixing but these are sitting directly on the burning flames. It makes cooking easier and faster so putting it all together is done within a few hours and nothing is wasted. It's also done as a self-serve. All the food is put onto different serving tables, and everyone gathers around the tables and takes what they want.

"The cooking continues as food needs to be replaced or it dries out and needs refreshing. There is a head chef and a sue chef, me. We oversee everything; the rest is done by the people in their positions as they have been hired. There is heavy drinking, which is served by several servers who keep everything refreshed and nothing is left unattended.

"It doesn't matter that too much drinking is done because this happens only in the later day. The early time servings are on one window table by the kitchen door and for two hours, when people decide to eat, they just walk in and serve themselves sit, eat, and go back to work. It's very unique and efficient. We are not busy until it's time to set up and then it's only for a few hours, that's the early time services.

"During the late day, though, it is totally different. We are busy the whole time because everyone eats big. This happens seven days a week. We do not serve breakfast that is everyone's own responsibility before coming to work. The Emperor's breakfast is made and served entirely by the kitchen staff."

"Interesting, and the Emperor sits where?" replied Je-hu.

"He doesn't, the only time he joins the rest of us is after an election, and because they have never served longer than two months, to date, and the latest one serving only a day, I don't know what the arrangements are. I only started two months before the last election," Nehan said.

"Oh. Well, that creates a bit of a dilemma. And that's your job, to find out where he is served, most important, what the special dishes are for him. There are other things as well but those two are number one on the list," Je-hu deliberated.

"Sora, tell me about your position and how it's worked," Je-hu asked.

"I'm in a different part of the kitchen though we are close to the kitchen, it's totally different. And we work in the earliest part of the day and finish just after lunch is served. We start with early buns, for the live-in staff and Emperor; there are only seven, three security guards and two groundskeepers, the chef and the Emperors aid.

"The breakfast takes one and a half hours then we start on the lunch, baking, desserts three kinds, buns and bread. That takes us about two to three hours depending on the menu and then the evening which is very extensive. We are usually finished by three or four in the afternoon," Sora explained.

“Wow, this work sounds more like a lifestyle than a job. People must be fighting to get into a position at the Emperor’s building,” Je-hu implied. “We need to hear from the janitors what are your names and what shift do you work.

“Aa-z and Raju,” said a soft indistinguishable voice from behind Sora, as he stepped into view he lit a gaff (cigarette). “I’m on the early day shift and the man, of not so many words, is on late days. He prefers it and he has seen some things that appear questionable. He’s bigger than me and can handle himself better.”

Aa-z explained, looking at him he wasn’t any more than one and a half metres tall, so he could understand why taking the early shift was less confrontational because the later shift dealt more with a full building.

“Raju, maybe you should explain some of what you’ve seen.”

Je-hu said looking him straight in the eyes.

Raju is a skinny waif with no muscle to his frame he was sitting on the floor and from there he looked smaller than he was. As he began to stand his size started to be seen and though not so much muscle as he was tall his voice made him even more impressive.

“It isn’t anything to really give an alarm to just yet but at certain times each evening and in the morning there are lights and noises that circle the grounds. I’m passing it off as the ground keepers; they work at night and act suspiciously secretive. They don’t let anyone into their zone or workload unless they really need the extra help. Then it’s just for that project and they’re gone. They are very efficient but, as I said, very secretive. We have a security guard in the mix and maybe he can impress you with more information.”

Raju ended his line of information and pointed at Yasir. Je-hu looked at him and pondering for a moment began to say “Hmmm, and if you could introduce yourself we would be open to anything, more that you could add to this information. And my questions to you are how long have you been with security there, and what are your reasons for joining this infiltration?” asked Je-hu.

“The name is Yasir, and to answer the first question five years, the second is simple. I have been through two terms, and have been with the building through a few circumstances. The first Emperor that I worked for lasted two months. He was found in his room and was killed in the same manner, Red Ires.

“From my understanding, it’s the way most of the Emperors have met their demise. There was no evidence of foul play. No one coming or going and the only things around him were dead red Ire and cheese. Blood cheese, the most expensive and the most sought after, rare, and only available to the elite, and those who can afford it.

"Criminals, whores and thieves have all had their fill of it. So it isn't limited to the hierarchy. I have my suspicions of how the Emperors are killed and wish to find the reason why, and who is responsible. So here I am, at your service and ready to be and player in this conspiracy, ours, as well as, theirs," Yasir added.

"As for the groundskeepers, they are harmless, as far as I have seen and observed, their big secret is an herb. Why are they out at late day, herb, the beams are to let each other know where they are at any time. So if there is any other disturbance, they are accounted for, and have alibis instead of lies," he answered.

"OK, then we're set, as far as it goes you don't associate, there is plenty of time, with the election to plan for. If there is to be any association let it happen casually, as an introduction for work assignments, or with proper introductions. There cannot be any reason for suspicion or we compromise the whole plan, as well as the elected hopeful.

"So, no fraternising with anyone on the inside, and especially amongst each other, that way if one is discovered the others are safe. We will not have another meeting like this. We will separate each meeting, and I won't be the only operative you will see. It will be with one another, and he is Tumi. Sora will be the connection to Tumi, is this understood?"

All agreed.

And Je-hu continued, "This meeting is adjourned and I would like everyone to leave separately as not to arouse suspicion.

Chapter 6
The Assault
No Way Out

Must you be in fantasy
Believing all the things you see
Life's pieces scatter the ground
None can go where you are now
Every day's a baseball game
Diamonds in your eye's
Stories heard are all the same
As each game begins again

Easy come easy go
Where does the wind blow
Swept into destiny evading reality
Watching from a distant row
Innings come and innings go
Now the game begins again
No way out no way in

High card low card
Diamonds in your eye's
Reaching across the table
After each winning hand

High ball low ball
Stoned through every play
Drinking to each
Endurance
Ghosts around the
Frame

Where does the time go
Day's slip right by
Stories told are all the same
As each game begins again
Watching from a distant row
Innings come and innings go
Is it that you just pretend
No way out now way in

“All right,” said Ohn-ohn.

As they lifted the ground cover to the portal, the air was musty and stale; there hangs a ladder, down to the floor below. Though deteriorated it wasn’t compromised much and could still hold weight but it had to be taken one at a time. They began their descent, Naveen was first, then Nayrr, Who stood at the bottom and caught the gear as Ohn-ohn lowered it.

Then it was Ohn-ohn’s turn, but as he descended one of the rungs snapped and, the length of rope that held everything together was more deteriorated than first perceived and broke. Ohn-ohn fell ten feet to the floor and something snapped a loud snap. As he tried to get up his face distorted from the pain, though he let out no sound, it, the pain, showed on his face.

“Well,” grimacing in pain, “I think I’ve broken my, my foot and not just the ankle, but the shin and several toes. Did anyone think to bring a tensor bandage?” asked Ohn-ohn.

Naveen reached into her bag and pulled out what Ohn-ohn needed, the break was not as bad as first thought and is more a minor fracture so wrapping it as tenderly as Naveen made sure it was tight as well as comfortable so that the circulation could continue and Ohn-ohn could still support weight on his leg. Ohn-ohn got up and tested his foot, it hurt but was not unbearable the toes and ankle were only sprained and the bandage would slow the swelling. He could still carry his equipment, which was a good thing because if it had to be left behind they would lose some very important pieces of their equipment. The escape corridor was built to withstand bombings and natural disasters, but it is also wider than the plans showed.

So it was easier to navigate, especially with all the equipment that was being carried. The stale air made it difficult to breathe and they all showed their fatigue. The walk to the wall of the building’s foundation took more time than anticipated due to the fall. The escape corridor, being ten feet below the ground, had no ventilation making the air a little thinner than expected.

As they came to the end of the corridor they touched a wall, a door, they could go no further, Ohn-ohn had been at this end of this entrance in the past and knew his way around it.

“Don’t touch anything,” whispered Ohn-ohn. “There are light beams all over the inside area and they are sensitive. There is another way in and it’s through the walls. It may take some time to find but it’s here that’s how I knew about this passage. Be patient, and it will be found, we have the whole five days to work with, so just relax."

Ohn-ohn went onto say, "It should be in the corner right about..."

The team set up the lighting units they had brought with them. Ohn-ohn started to feel for a grooved seam in the corner where the wall intersected with thc corridor. Because of his compromised foot, Ohn-ohn needed Nayrrs help to open the crook and because it hadn't been used for decades it was very tight and needed some pounding on each joint and hinge. After an hour of pushing and working, the entrance, it finally gave enough space to let them through.

Surprisingly, there was a staircase between the walls, like a separation between rooms but with more width like a secret entrance, which led to the floor they wanted, finding a ventilation screen they could see into the area giving them an overview of the whole level. It was an open area floor and the lighting was enough to be able to make out every room. Though separated alphabetically and by district the person, we needed was still going to be a tough find.

But the first thing was to get past the light beams and take themselves out to make it easier to move freely and without setting off any alarms. The way this had to be done is to scale the walls and find the electrical leads to the cameras, the beams and the locking systems to each room on each floor.

The architecture of this building is based on new tech and old foundation. It was one of the first to be redefined with a different technique to seal the walls of the exterior and redesign the interior with a new structure. There are four outer towers; they are forty-eight metres high, at each corner, attached to the original foundation. The foundation is formed as one solid piece from the mountain rock.

The towers are made of steel, smooth for forty-two metres; the last six metres are glass structures, to form the peak of each tower. From each corner of the outer towers, in length, it is one hundred metres, in width it is fifty meters. Then there are four inner towers, these towers stand at sixty metres, each outer and inner tower is a staircase and can be entered from any floor, so we cannot use them it would be too obvious.

Because the technology is so new, when they decided to use this building as the guinea pig, a simple use in the reconstruction was decided for visual perspective and caution. The seal, between the glass, is a frame and is held together by magnetism, this is a new idea that needed to be tested in actual practice. The exterior glass is mirrored and, in some sections frosted this prevents people from seeing what's inside and reflects light to keep the building cool and adds architectural style.

"Triple-A, this is better than we could have hoped for, everything is glassed and named so finding the right room will be easier and we can keep in sight of each other and know what each of us is doing," said Ohn-ohn.

The floor we need to be on is the second, inside frosting and colour is used extensively as a separation of rooms, for separation of county, provinces and states.

The states are the areas outside the borders of Kranaqus.

"The first thing we have to do is turn off the alarms, Nayrr, have you got the white-out? We have to find the electrical system before we access the level we need. I know it's on the first level but where the wiring comes into the building isn't where we need to look," Ohn-ohn said while looking through the electrical page.

"From where we are the electrical circuit is on the other side of the building. Are there other passages that follow the walls in order to make finding the electrical circuit easier? I hope they thought about maintenance and kept everything accessible," replied Nayrr.

"Yes, there are passages but only around the old foundation, luckily, but it will be tight with this equipment. We are in the right corridor, and the second-level drop is three metres below us on an adjoining tunnel so getting to that area is going to be tough, the screen just behind Naveen is where we enter. Once we are on the other side," Ohn-ohn pointed out. "It will be at the top of the wall, below the light fixture."

Then they jumped down to the next corridor.

"What's our next move?" asked Naveen.

"Well, these corridors span around the whole foundation, there are four exit tunnels and ten doors into them from various locations inside the building. As you can see this one continues around the eastern tower and onto the next doors that enter inside. Right now we are just below ground level, and when we get into the front entrance, it drops down again another three metres." Ohn-ohn described. "When we get to the other side we enter through one of the doors and start scaling walls."

Getting to the third drop went smooth, but as the team reached the front of the building Naveen tripped and fell against Ohn-ohn who then pounded his broken ankle to the floor. He let out a horrific painful scream.

"Well, that's one way to find the hatch," Nayrr remarked, holding back a laugh.

After Ohn-ohn regained his composure, looking right into Nayrr eyes, he said, "This is a very important mission, yet, you seem to find humour. I can now not continue. You have to go on, on your own."

"So that's where we are then, In the middle of this and without our inside man," Nayrr said turning and standing over Ohn-ohn. He then went down to the next level barking at Naveen.

"Step on it, we are the only two and have less time than you think."

Joining Nayrr, Naveen and he went over the bags and put together only the essential items and continued down to the end of the second corridor. Setting up the lighting they began studying the wall into the first floor that would put them one metre from the ceiling.

"Have you got the charges?" Nayrr asked as he pulled out the little capsules of powder and a laser drill.

"This drill is accurate within a microunit. We are only going to free them so the bricks can be replaced, enough for the door on the other side to be extracted, we can only hope the drawing is accurate."

Nayrr started measuring from the corridor end wall to the middle of the brick wall and drew a centre vertical line. The door to the escape stairwell is only two feet wide, so the removal should be a narrow one. The charges are not big; all they need to do is fracture the mortar so the bricks can be removed.

It took several hours to set the charges and remove the bricks. Opening the door was a little difficult as they haven't been touched in, at least, fifteen years. Nayrr, set out the hangers to take a seat under the light fixture, for working with the breaker system and disrupt it. They discovered that scaling the walls was unnecessary; there is a service screen on the second floor, while Naveen entered the second floor by using the service entrance above the light fixture.

Nayrr crawled up after he was finished; Naveen heard him say, "Just as I suspected, reverse design. This is not a problem, I have turned off all the electronics on this floor everything was separated and there was a map left inside the box with the exact electrical plans to follow. We just have to get through the division doors to find the right rooms to focus on."

As Naveen checked the door she discovered it locked "Hey, Nayrr, this door is still locked."

“Yes, expected, but there is a trick Ohn-ohn told me of,” Nayrr reached under the threshold and flicked the latch holding the lock. Swinging the door open he bowed and gestured, to Naveen, to enter, holding his fingers to his lips, Nayrr remarked “there are audio detectors everywhere, do you know what room you’re looking for?”

She nodded yes.

“Good, just go and we’ll meet back here. We have three days” Naveen continued to room two and headed to ‘Life Active’ file cabinet one through nine and started.

Nayrr proceeded to historical; he was given the job of finding the extra files to each of the “Concealed Society Members” of the committee to the Emperor. This room was a little harder to find. It seemed an hour before stumbling onto its entrance, it was found camouflaged as part of the wall on the end of the corridor. It is a tight entrance but once inside, the room was a vast where the house of filing, by rotations and decades. But he knows what he’s looking for, last year of the longest term of an Emperor in power.

“Not an easy find,” he thought while walking the isles.

The ceilings are so high that the steel shelving is comfortable at six metres high. He looked around and, in his travels, found a levitation platform, it was on charge on the far wall.

“This will make my search much faster. I hope Naveen found just such a craft,” he said aloud.

As he studied the controls with the instructions given on the wall, he stepped on the board and started moving through the aisles. He discovered two books at the top of one of the shelving racks one titled “REGIONAL AFFAIRS” and the other titled “EMPERORS A HISTORY” they weren’t dusty so they obviously are still in use and have been used recently. Pages, from the beginning to the end could be taken out or added at will. By the looks of them, though, they looked unmolested from their fabrication and they are huge, and one of them is open.

“REGIONAL AFFAIRS” has new entries. It’s about the coming election, there are dates of campaigning parties, names of the different committees of volunteers, names and addresses of the elected members and running offices, there are the names of the running candidates their addresses, education and medical histories. This is all from the last election, for the Emperor. While reading through he found the names of each acting council member at this time. And looking deeper into the book there it was, the Emperor who last held a long term. His name is unimportant; it's the committee members that are needed. To compare the list against who represents the Emperor now, the timeline is very short in terms of the elected, short term, Emperors, twenty-six years.

"This is very suspicious," thought Nayrr, to himself, no wonder he wants these profiles.

"*I'm not an investigator, but as I go backwards into the book, it is very clear how the power has changed. When reading through the long-term seat there were many changes to the Emperor's council and the seats that occupied it.*" As he reviewed the records.

After the council has gone through a reorder of seats and shifting power, there has been little change to the board of directors, and the committee members have been very consistent, but the Emperors have all suffered loss of life in many different ways, which all are made to seem like accidents. But the last two, because of their similarities, tell a different story. "*I can see the conspiracy here,*" Nayrr thought.

Finding the board members is going to be easy, everything is captioned with catalogue and file no. for reference and placement. All he was asked to get is the comity profiles, but in studying the information it is apparent to Nayrr that the board of directors and the council of legalities is just as important to have, so he took all the names down and proceeded to find every profile of recent membership.

Even though he had all the locations where to find each folder it was still a difficult task. They were scattered all over each section by region, not by seat or membership. Personal history stayed with where they started from and when occupying a new position a new folder would be opened and past history would not follow including Medical. In order to get everything Nayrr would have to go to the "LIVES ACTIVE "files to get all the profile information on each member," this is a big job, it's good that we have three days," thought Nayrr, to himself. "I wonder how Naveen is doing" and he went to find her.

Chapter 7
The Committee

Little Risk'e

Your walk your talk
The way you move
The way you strut
Your style your eyes
The look of lust
In the night
Too mean to cool
Feel the heat from
The city little risk'e

You lie cheat and steel
Love behind the wheel
Sunset till dawn
It's what makes you
Feel better
No reason no time
In and out makes it right
Little risk'e

Your style your wild
The things you say
Make it right
The streets the lights
To mean to cool
Doing whatever
Makes you feel better
Little risk'e

Just a little risk'e business
What's your pleasure
Neon's treasure

You get all you need
As you walk a neon beat
The love I seek
Can't hide from me
You get what you want
And I get what I need
The love I seek
Can't escape my seed
Lady

Politically, Kranaqus society is arranged in this likeness, there are elected bodies in each district, and from each area, there forms a council of five. From each council, there is one committee representative, which then forms a committee of five. They then regulate the elected bodies that govern over the people.

The emperor is the only representative who can overrule (veto) the committee of five, by veto, the citizens vote the emperor in but, the elected MG (ministers of government) run the people, in their riding. In it there is deceit and corruption. Spies are always in the wing and threaten the inner core which can lead to mistrust, deceit, shame and expulsion.

Torture is always a scare tactic used to keep citizens in their place and sway voters, to vote in the favour of the favourite to win elections. But it, torture, is not something that most belief happens, and there is no proof of its use. But, sometimes candidates just disappear and are never seen again. This brings suspicion of the use of torture, in the political forum, into the race to become governor.

The power the governors wield is great. Everything goes through their administrations, nothing is overlooked, and if one is caught in deceit or smuggling, it could lead to long term prison sentences or death. Depending on what it is being smuggled, or whom you were deceiving the citizen may just disappear.

Elections happen often but are in general, once every ten rotations, upon the death of an MG (minister of government), or a coup, which is a regular occurrence. There are long sitting MG members, but they are well guarded and have made very close ties to the committee, but for the most part of the riding, especially in the sub-municipalities and rural communities, no one can trust their position to be long term without securities and heavy backing from the citizens.

The committee is made up of five; they are elected in by the MG members and are lifetime. They represent the Emperor and are his trusted counsel to inform and direct him with decisions and new law. Overseeing the administration of MG in the province, making sure all counties abide by the old and the new laws and ordinances put into place by committee or MG members. The committee direction is to the MG members who then administer the rulings to the citizens.

Keeping order is difficult every clan wants someone to represent them in government, no matter how small their family is, being an MG member gives them ultimate power over all citizens. They can appropriate land for their own use, as long as it is for municipal, or governing purposes, such as; community halls, administration buildings, transportation depots, roads and so on.

When hiring staff it is generally done within their own clan, that way trust issues are not a concern. Because of rumours of torture in the governing clans, trust is a very important business concern. The use of torture has only been suggested as a use by the committee closest to the Emperor, but there have been hints of its use with all MG members. This has never been proven because no one has come out alive to accuse or offer witnessed testimony.

1. There is a drug made from a fish, the blowfish (pufferfish), on the world of Devi, its poison, a sack taken after death and then dried, is blown into the face of the intended victim breathed in and then attacks the nervous system and renders the individual motionless (in a state of hyper suspended animation) yet he/she still can see, hear and know what is going on around them but cannot respond. The person is then placed on a stainless-steel table and cut from the anise, through the groin, up the torso disembowelling the subject. The breast bones do not need to be touched but the skin is sliced to the neck and then inserted into the larynx and cut just under the chin.
   Adam's apple is then removed and skidded across the table to the edge to drop onto the floor. All this is done while the person is alive and unable to move or do anything about this procedure. All that can be done is watch while their organs spill onto the table as the life of the individual slowly drains. Death is the only solace. Before the procedure, there is only one question to be answered: does the joystick stay whole or is it divided in half, while separating the testicles?
2. Being slowly cut to pieces, this is used to extract information about conspirators, coups and possible assassinations. When the person of question is brought in, to be questioned, he/she is first threatened with the idea of losing pieces of body parts if they are not cooperative. If the agents have to resort to amputation before the information is given, then that citizen has signed their death warrant.
3. Beatings, anatomical probing and wet ropes being tied to a chair or table while having blunt instruments slammed down on their body. Then, after it is determined that all has been extracted the citizen is lobotomised.

4. Shock torture: bringing together electrical cables and laying them on different parts of the body, touching and inserting, to create burns inside and out.

Microwaves are also used for this same purpose. Lobotomising is also the end result of this torture as well.

These are just four of the tortures that have been known to be used. There is a book of torture methodology, heard through the grapevine of estate workers who have been told by long term employees. There is no documentation, no eyewitnesses and only theorised that it's done as a way of getting rid of political oppositions and suspected spies.

Spies are not uncommon but when accused it's most often being in the wrong place at the wrong time. So it's always best to just do the job you are assigned to and not loiter, or act suspicious outside the work environment.

Person of interest: opposition lead candidate, running elected to hold office

Committee Members

(THSOT)

The Historical Society of Technology, also known as "The Committee"

Fanyrottiss: A tall arrogant male with high expectation of compliance always the centre of attention.

Harour: A short but stout individual has a lot to say but never seems to be heard.

Axyan: Always gets in what he wants to say and is agreeable to everything done and said by Fanyrottiss.

Misric: A short fat, almost obese arrogant in a standoffish way.

Umutt: Short plump unseen and never really heard but arrogant always has something to add or say.

Chapter 8

Sora entered the bakery.

"Where have you been," the head baker roared. "We have a lot to do and, without a full staff, time will be limited."

The head baker is a short plump, tailless, man who ran the bakery like a military camp.

"Ahhh, your record has been spotless why have you chosen such a day to be tardy? You're being promoted to serve/helper. Your first assignment, being that you are so late, is to serve breakfast. You're too late to help with preparation."

Turning to face Sora, he barrelled out, "So get into the proper attire and start serving the morning meal. You will be setting the serving carts and taking them to the committee members. After that, you will begin your training."

Sora entered the kitchen, went into the cloakroom to get changed. The committee members are the only guests, in the estate. They have the run of the Emperors estate upon leave of absence or Death. The families of the committee also live in the estate.

As long as the committee is in power they can make laws, set rules as they see fit and govern the state without question. They have the complete power of attorney until a new Emperor is elected. Changes in the committee only happen due to death, dismissal, misappropriation, obstruction, or to obtain more power.

Her wardrobe seemed a little tight and short, if she did anything too fast, bend over to serve or stretched in any way she was sure it would tear and fall off of her tight little body. When Sora looked at what was being served and how much of it was going to each room, actually it is a villa and each member lived in separate units, she was surprised that one could eat so much. But, she soon discovered every meal feeds the whole family, so she realised that it is at least a two-hour serving time. There are only two servings throughout the day, morning and evening, lunch is a buffet and served in the dining area for all staff and committee members.

Although the day was a blustery one, Sora was not discouraged; the villa is undercover so the weather did not affect anyone walking through or around the estate. The business didn't start until 10:00 am and the first serving cart is sent out at 6:30 am so everyone is completed by 8:30 am. They are given one and a half hours to eat, cart pick up is at 10:00, if the cart is not outside the door for pickup then it is up to a family member to take it to the kitchen.

Of the five members, there were only two families in the villa, so it took only twenty minutes to deliver the carts. Then she went to the board room, for the first of her nine sessions of training classes that were to be taken over the next five months.

Sora had two sit-ins, one hour for each, one after breakfast and the other before going home. Walking into the boardroom Sora glanced at the table, big enough to seat fifteen, she couldn't stop herself from reading some of the paperwork on it. The first page she picked up was a set of guild rules of the kitchen outlining the responsibilities of each position starting with the chef, as she turned the pages and found her title. Server/kitchen help, she took a booklet and sat down.

Reading through the agenda she saw that her duties were very tight.

- Prepping for the morning
- Setting out dishes
- Making sure all carts were well stocked
  Serving the carts to each townhouse
- Cleaning the kitchen area
- Returning with the breakfast carts
- Clean down for the next shift

Yasir entered the room, "Have you been entered into the security files yet?" he questioned.

"No," Sora replied.

"Well, come with me, we need to take fingerprints, hair samples, pictures and you need to fill out some forms. Everyone goes through this.

It's routine. Then you come back for the presentation to your assigned position."

Sora followed him down to the security office and went through the routine of profile entry. This took an hour and then went back to the conference room and again waited. She sat there for at least twenty minutes before the sous chef entered and demanded to know what she was doing.

"What are you doing just sitting around? Don't you know there is work to be done?" he roared.

"I was told by the chef to come here and wait."

"Did security come?"

"Yes, get back into the kitchen there is major prep to be done before the next shift," he bellowed. And she got up and went in to face the chef.

Estate spies

Yasir: Security
Aa-z: Janitor
Raju: Janitor
Sora: Team leader/kitchen help, server
Nehan: Sue chef
Je-hu: Light Streamer
Nayrr: Outside contact

Chapter 9
Silent Running

And moving on through the years
What changes do we find
And challenges that bind us
Do they help pass the time
As life around us carries on
And as we each fall in love

Reaching to hold a hand
Is it met half way
Finding there is and there is not
Time to turn away
It is within us all
The gift of life
The thought of death
To contemplate it's unknown
Who it is we come to know

Silent running
A drift in the night
Silent running
Instilled in flight
Silent running
With love there is life
With knowledge we create
Then again explore it

And there you sit
No thoughts on mind
Look into
Late night skies
Empty thoughts
Escape us all
To contemplate and
Come to know
Where it is we will roam
And where it is we call home

"I have brought you in today privately to show you what we have discovered about our universe and what we believe to be true from observation at the borders of our universe," Je-hu exclaimed as he motioned Tumi to set a game of Campaigne.

This new technology your world has begun to use will cultivate and your people will begin to think beyond your atmosphere. Right now there is little or no consideration to technology that would take your citizens above and outside the security of your planet, but that will change and you will be a part of it and also direct it. This technology is very dangerous in the wrong hands and right now the committee, in place, is the wrong participants. We will guide you and direct your growth.

We are not going to speed you into a technological advancement but more act as a supporter." Je-hu expressed,

"The size of your planet has the richness, of minerals, that are needed to make this technology possible. It will be a good exchange to have your planets interact with ours for trade and growth. The resources of your planet, that we mine, will bring new industry and development to the citizens and the rewards will be felt throughout the whole of your world," Je-hu said with encouragement.

"What of the members of the committee, do we keep them alive or are they dispensable?" Tumi enquired.

"They will undoubtedly have secrets, places they have hidden valuables as well as technological advancements that we will need to know of. I would suggest that at least one remain alive to give us insight into their hidden assets and engineering."

Je-hu continued, "I would like to let you know what we have discovered.

Bubbles and Balloons

It was once thought that, in the idea of positive and negative, matter and antimatter (dark Matter) were somehow connected, without one there could not be the other. This is true. It was also thought that dark matter would be found in inner space, this is true as well, but with new technology and the ability to travel to the edge of the known universe, which is all there is, it became known that dark matter is not just inside but outside the universe bubble. A theorist once said, if you look at a bubble and impress yourself on its shape, size and form, what gives it, its life? Is it what's inside this form, or what's outside this form, or could it be what makes it a form? Which brings to question, what makes this a form at all? Theorists pondered this thought for many rotations and came to the conclusion that the only way they could answer the question is to go there.

The new technology allowed this, when they came to the wall it was dark and, what looked like emptiness, was actually liquid. There is a mathematical formula behind this discovery (the God Equation) but that will be made known later. What is on the other side, or what they were staring at is what holds the universe together.

Dark Matter, they also discovered, when looking back at the inner body of space, there was no expansion going on at all, instead it was circling giving the illusion of expansion. What does this mean? Everything is absolute. There is only inner rotation and rogue exodus to nova and supernova, but this is also absolute. As well blue stars are sometimes wandering rogues but still maintain an orbiting path.

The dark matter of Inner space is what holds a fixed cluster together but it also, upon discovery with our travels throughout the universe; they are the wormholes that allow this travel to be. They create a time displacement that can be manipulated for time travel, forwards and backwards. This displacement creates time relativity so there is no losing time placement when travelling. We can be kept in relative time to every period of expected difference between worlds and galaxies.

The conclusion they came to is this. When looking at a body of water what do you see? A flowing opulence of life, a liquid of creation, or a body of decay, what is it?

We can explain it by observation when taking a bubble bath, doing dishes, or pouring a soda, the bubbles you see are in the simulation of creation. Inside those bubbles, there may not be an activity, but this is questionable. What is keeping these forms from imploding? It might be the inside activity, but I suggest that it is the outside wall that holds the form of the bubble.

Just as a balloon is the protective shield of its inner space, and everything inside generates the length of the bubbles time in the form. In other words, it creates the size of the bubble, not the holding power. It's what is outside the inner activity of its inner space that keeps the bubble in the shape that it holds. In another sense, the balloon wall is dark matter. Dark Matter forms the wall that separates the outer space from the inner space, of the bubble, as a protecting wall or barrier.

From another point of view, when observing bubbles and their behaviour what is the first observation made? Bubbles always rise and float on the surface of the liquid or fluid that created them. What if, the bubbles that rise to the top of the liquid are not life-supporting entities but barren, and only the bubbles that are equal to the pressure of the liquid remaining below the surface are capable of supporting life. These are few in a pool of many floaters.

How many bubbles are life-supporting? This is the question that remains redundant as we cannot know how many bubbles are floating at any time. So we can honestly say at least one, ours.

How many liquid pools are there? That is a question that remains latent, as we are not capable of knowing such information. We can only surmise the existence of these pools for we are microbes in size and trapped in its creation, 'Our universe'.

Bubbles: When looking at bubbles and how they are formed what observation is made, it takes a combination of liquids to form bubbles. They can be formed singularly or multiple. Singular, through the source of a circular device, blowing into it with an air hose or, with your own breath produces a bubble that lasts seconds or minutes depending on the inner and outer pressures.

In other words, the inner stability of gravitational force to the outer stability of the liquid, producing the barrier of the bubble wall, or God Barrier, this wall has created, in essence, it would create a sustainable balance of energy and keep the outer wall (God Barrier) from collapse, giving the bubble a longer duration and act as a life force to the inner space of energy.

By observing bubbles in a pool of water it can be seen that some bubbles last longer than others. How does this occur?

It can only be suggested that there is an inner force allowing this to happen. And that the outer wall governs its time by the strength of endurance and depth in the liquid pool. The formation of these bubbles shows that each bubble mass is surrounded by a foamy substance thereby reinforcing each wall that creates the bubble mass. This suggests that a universe can have the same formation from its creation source, giving a longer life span to the bubble mass of the universe to support inner energy of space that is life creating.

As time moves forward the bubble mass becomes less, what we can conclude is lifelessness, which means that each bubbles inner energy has collapsed as there is no inner resource to keep it strong and the outer wall becomes too heavy to hold in place. Everything then resolves to its creation pool except that that holds a strong enough energy to subsist and have the possibility of its own creative energy. Then the process begins again, on what level is unknown, but the dishes have to be done again and things have to be cleaned, so it all begins again and again.

Balloons can also provide an insight into the God Barrier and a universe life cycle. A balloon, when blown up, has an inside pressure that keeps it inflated, this is a simulation of an acting god barrier separating inner and outer space, outer space, being the void or god pool. These two areas act in concert with each other and the wall separating them creates a barrier that has an infinite border between the inner and outer pressures that are in continuous flux.

As one watches a balloon, over a period of days, it deflates, thus showing that there are minute holes in the fabric of its form. There is no inner movement to create a constant force (referred to as universal gravity) to make an opposing force that balances the outer force of the god pool or the void.

If it is a void then the universes inner pressure is not countered by an outer space of emptiness and the action of the god barrier, acting as the sustaining factor holding the universal governing force or gravity together as it floats through the emptiness. This is created by contentious motion, without this inner movement there would be no pressure acting on the barrier, and like the balloon, it would collapse into itself imploding to nonexistence.

Yet there is flux. This is caused by unsteady pressures and shifting forces around the inner barrier. The inner force is created by the life force of energy made by their existence.

This tells us that there is an outer pressure giving stronger evidence to an outer pool (God Pool) with a constant force of pressure and an understanding of drifting in a pool rather than floating through a void. Without the inner gravitation of substance, for example, galaxies, solar systems of planets and the energy it generates, which create the pressure as a result of the movement of galaxies to produce the life that we know exists. But as we look into the darkness of space we see many forms and formations, and only by observation can we conclude that we are not alone.

Our deep thinkers always thought that dark matter was adrift in inner space and that it periodically would collide with each other causing a concussion that is difficult to detect. But when thinking about outer space (space outside the God Barrier) and comparing it to the idea of a balloon, as a simulation, by putting them in the same perspective as an example, we can use the balloon as the dark matter barrier (God Barrier), and by using two balloons to simulate a collision, we could then examine how they perform and assume that dark matter would act in the same manner.

We could also look around and use examples of collisions, by force of nature, or invention, automobiles, hurricanes, storms, tornadoes and so on. and realise that dark matter is not the object of the collision, but the concussion caused by the impact. In other words, the pressure created by two opposing forces, and the governing barrier that keeps them separated.

This, we have discovered, is how dark matter is detected, with the destruction of the structure. It is with the structure that acts as the barrier between spaces but can only be assumed to be dark matter upon entering its inner space. So we are not working with the collision itself but the concussion as a result of the impact or destruction.

Chapter 9a
(Gravity)
Bubbles and Balloons

The balance between the God barrier and inner space is governed by the rotation of the universe. It creates a force that keeps all things in balance and separated. Centrifugal forces are these alliances to the illusion of expansion, but it is only within a parameter of the energy released by its source, for example, nova versus supernova, creation of stars, planets, life.

We assume that all things are connected by energy, it has an element of truth but energy is not without its own connection to universal power. When one looks into Quantum physics to observe a nucleus surrounded by electrons, what holds these particles together? Gravity is the ultimate source of energy, without it, nothing would be congruent. Without the emptiness of space there would be no room for formation, and yet, there is so much matter that without the dearth of stars and planetary systems new life could not be created. The role of gravity is universal, our bubble called "the universe", has a central part as a whole. Without the gravitational force of the universe, created by galaxies, nothing would exist in its space.

How is this known?

By observing thc formation of stars we see clockwise and counter clockwise movement, relating to creation. This is how life around this phenomenon happens, the question is, which of the systems is life creating, clockwise or anti-clockwise? By observation over a five-millennium period anticlockwise has a faster life-giving resource, while clockwise time does create life, but it has a long time before creation, due to synchronised movement with the universe. One would think otherwise but clockwise time remains constant, while with anti-clockwise movements time remains in flux and gives a greater resource to life.

Anti-clockwise movement creates a real-time factor of progression, where clockwise time can remain stagnant. It has been discovered that clockwise movement creates less friction and therefore has very little resistance to give the formed system a known presence, and the force of life can remain dormant.

Looking at the rotation of tires on a car, as they move in a counter clockwise direction, when observing them on camera they can appear to be moving in a clockwise direction, and they are, but they are not. This contradiction keeps the forces of motion in order, by countering the directional energy of the motion it remains constant, yet in flux. This is a natural alliance with gravity. This is referred to as chaotic order, like the turmoil inside a hurricane. The eye of the hurricane is the order inside its chaos.

When observing the rotation of the universe it moves in a clockwise direction giving the illusion of expansion. So it only goes to suggest that planetary systems would be countering that direction to maintain an orbit around a governing body (star).

In the context of universal movement, the element of time and speed is the structure of the flow. Everything has a flow within the movement of the universal gravity bond. When looking at different solar orbits in a governing system of planetary bodies rotating around a star, constant movement is relative to the universe's gravitation of force and energy. We have observed that the distance of solar movement is relative to the movement of the universe's rotation in distance.

Though it is fractional, considering the size of its bubble, the rotation of every orbiting system emulates the universal movement in time and distance over speed.

Like the movement of a watch everything must remain in sync or it will become skewed and then loses or gains time depending on its chaotic movement, if this occurs, life-giving substance remains dormant, this happens as a result of fluctuating temperatures and unstable rotation. The north and south polar stability also play a part in a life-giving source.

If there is too much movement with the polar caps, the star's energy cannot be constant, unless there is more than one star. This can help make life happen, but it would be in constant beginnings, or in other words, starting over and over without reaching a foothold, then stagnate into a drone, with no evolutionary growth.

Plant life remains at an unstable stage of infancy. This could mean that it remains as an oceanic consign with no or little exposure to land life, keeping everything in its beginning stages, stagnating all forms of advancement.

The discovery has also been made of asteroid and satellite (moons) life forming bodies. This happens at a more frequent level than first thought. Undeveloped planets can act like suns and provide enough radiance to create life on orbiting satellites.

The one factor is the evolution of such a happening is also measured by the orbit of the moon to the planet and the planet to the star. There cannot be an offset of time between the planet to star constant, and the moon to planet orbit. This means that not only does the rotation have to remain constant and emulate the same distance as from the sun in the percentage of size and orbit, but planetary temperature.

As well as maintain a gravitational equilibrium from the planet to star constant. Without this there would be no congruence and life would not evolve. The satellite would continue to remain in stagnated infancy or not go on, and just begin over and over again at each optimum interval (planet and moon in balance with distance, temperature and planetary stability) remaining in a state of idleness. An asteroid can be acted on by both sun and planet this would give it a much stronger resource to create life. But it is rare.

We have had great theorists and thinkers explain their ideals and equations to our scientists for many millennia. Until the discovery of a technology that changed the old thinking into a new construct and ideology, nothing has ever been proven, "The God equation" there will be more on this equation in later books.

Nothing

Where nothing comes nothing goes
If nothings dreamed nothings bestowed
As nothing wants nothing has
Where nothing is love is found

As nothing gets nothing gives
Where nothings seen nothing is
If nothings said nothings known
What nothing wants is nothing at all

When nothings dealt nothing folds
If nothing breeds nothing lives
As nothings shipped nothing sells
Where nothing is love is found

Found by those
Who've crossed the line
Those of whom are
Trapped in time
Found by those
Who've yet to find
Those of you
Whom are trapped in mind

Chapter 9b
(God Pool)
Bubbles and Balloons

God pools are many, some are dormant, some are sterile, others are life-giving. This means that they are ready for universe creation but need the fluid of another resource to create. God pools are not equal. Only some have the ability to create bubbles of living universes. Many bubbles can be formed but it is only within certain types of composition that life-giving bubbles are created.

Contrary to an earlier period, where a big bang was the result of universe creation, we have established that creation happens with a whisper, from a splash. As a faucet pours water into a basin a splash occurs. If there is no substance for creation then it remains dormant or in other words just rippling fluids across a pool of suppressed liquid of always. Many bubbles can be formed but it takes a special combination of events to activity.

Yet, when influenced by embryonic fluids from another source (God Pool) Bubbles will occur and life forces can be a part of the generating universes, but not give a life substance of the order. It cannot be known, without experiment. What type of formula would impress an undertaking of this kind? How many pools are needed to influence a life-giving universe is this question for discussion or a theory for the experiment.

There is no way of knowing without someone's curiosity. So all that can be said is whisper, splash, explosion, or all three combined, until it is challenged, with experimentation, there is no one method of action or thought to life-giving universe life happenings. One can only say "it occurs". As an example; when running water hits straight water with no enhancing substances little or nothing occurs, but when an enhancement is added we get bubbles.

That is how a god pool, hypothetically, functions to produce bubbles of multiple universes, dormant, sterile, or life-supporting. How do we know this to be true? We don't, but it can be surmised that one God pool could not create without the influence of another. Therefore, it can be suggested, the development of many god pools, as a resource of essence or substance by pouring into, or the mixture of, from one or many, creates the bubbles that will eventually be many living universes or a single universe.

By holding a balloon, after blowing it up, when the condensation begins to gather you could say life is in there. Could we not? As the warmth of the sun heats the balloon it can expand or just stay the same until the fluid evaporates, the balloon then begins to implode and at that moment everything that died.

When rubbing the balloon on your hair there forms an electrical charge that helps to keep it connected to a stationary source this creates a form of gravity and sometimes, when overcharged, will combust. This gives one the idea of different stages of universe collapse. Also, it can be an example of phases of universe status, expansion and/or stability.

In Closing

When we think of dark matter we can only assume its existence, we can also say it's all around us, by observing the life force of animate to inanimate we can suggest that any time an entity enters a space the framework of that space is the dark matter of the inner space of the structure. Such as a car, a house, an aeroplane, a boat these form the barriers of outer space and inner space. If one wants to measure its force strength, by colliding it into a similar structure or an immovable or stationary force or structure the energy of its collision is the measurement of the dark matter barrier.

Chapter 10
Naveen

As Naveen entered room two, right at the entrance, she found a levitation craft plugged into the charger.

"How convenient," she said aloud and began observing the control arm.

She then stepped on the platform and it turned on automatically. By playing with the handle, she discovered how to make it rise and fall, and with varying speeds, it took her throughout the room quickly. The room is very large and difficult to manage but she had been on one of these a few times while on the outer face of the mount. Sheer, which is the highest peak and has the longest face of any slope of all the mountain ranges on Qua.

She took it to the top of the first row to get an overall view and was stupefied by the vastness of shelving, "*No wonder*", she thought, referring to the levitation device she stood on. While scanning the shelving units she noticed, in the far corner, three books set at the top of the bookcase and headed to them to find out what they could be of.

Standing over them they each had their own titles, 'regional populations', 'births and deaths' and finally 'political enrolment, state and municipal'.

"Well, this is going to make it easier, not necessarily faster but, because it's put together by region of state and location to area, finding what I need will be much simpler," she thought aloud and caught herself, remembering what Ohn-ohn said just before separating, 'No talking aloud'.

Opening "Regional Populations" and combing through it she could read that it is, by location of the state, township and date, that she needed this book for reference to the date of birth. So she kept it open to the regional area she knew had a higher significance to who she would be looking for. Being in the medical field she has the knowledge of the percentage of the population that is compromised with diseases, birth defects, immunities and allergies. This understanding is limited to a small population and only given to medical authorities, of which she happens to be one.

Red Ires only live in the lower regions of the continent; therefore, only the towns and villages above 1,500 feet from sea elevations are needed to find this special person, Under "Political Enrolment" twenty-five years from this current date. Not difficult.

She opened births, so, there are five mountainous regions and within each region. Opening the "Political Enrolment" to upper regional districts: "These are all populated districts, above 1,500 feet, there are enough people to choose from, even though this disability is rare, the consideration of finding such people would be in a place where there is very little to no contact, with the species at all. There are 157 towns and villages." She stood thinking while turning pages to the most populated.

"I'm going to start with the densest and work my way to the outer, less populated areas."

While combing through the names of the recent entries she noticed that they were not in alphabetical order or by state but by elevation and region, ends up being very similar to state location anyway and puts everyone she is looking for at a glance. There seems to be an unrealistic amount of new listings. But she knows what she is looking for, and in the highest regions, there are hundred candidates, listed by name, address, and birthdate.

After writing all the names, she separated the names by the altitude of each address and by township or village, that way she wouldn't have to run all over the records for each name. Naveen knows this because she worked as a travelling medic for five years. Every time a position is changed the minimum hold of it is five years before considering a new position. So she got to know the layout of the higher Empire very well.

Naveen proceeded to the archives to get a look at every medical history. It's a process of elimination. Looking at her timepiece she realised she has two and a half days left, break time.

After an hour, or so, she looked at the regional map and found three mountains above 3,500 feet mount Kaya, the highest at 15,000 feet above water level. Ockuyu stands at 14,500 feet, and Pazar "the twins" at 75,000 feet.

"*Where, am I to begin*?" She thought. "The twins" seeing that it has the highest population compared to the other two, she will leave them until last.

"To start at the top, I am only looking for political entries" juggling and shuffling through the files. She's a fast reader when it comes to files, and in that area, there are ten well-populated towns, and after thorough examination, she found two candidates. They are in two different offices but on the same mountain and in the town of Quirec in the mountain range of Kaya. They will obviously know each other and will be difficult to keep from confrontation.

Their ideologies differ extremely yet they are opposed to the committee overseeing as the governing source and are very outspoken about it. Then she started on Ockuyu and there are two towns that stand out in elevation one, Winog is actually a village, but with four jurisdictions, the other Gwennole, which, as a town, has more municipal offices making the search a little harder. So she began looking and in each of them, she found one.

So now she has to move lower. This proved to be much harder than the first four candidates. There are many more areas that are populated and more separated. And it's proving to be difficult. So, it's also time for a break.

Finding the final person took longer than she thought it would be, but expected.

And just on the deadline. I knew Ohn-ohn was watching me for at least one hour or so and I thought he was about to ask if he could help, but probably thought better of it.

Naveen then started on the lower towns, under 4,500 feet, but sticking to a high elevation and in two of the high townships she found three more candidates, two in Menhir and one in Ysolda. They are in the mountain range of Pazar. So, rather than be shortlisted, she took all three names to research. Making seven in the mix Naveen started on to the medical records. Like everything, there is alphabetically sorted the members of parliament and municipalities are all separated, under civil, for the people.

Ministries: for the municipal, elected federal and members of parliament. She has found all the candidates that she thinks are the most eligible and puts them in the bag, then starts for the door, just as Tumi strolled into the room.

Mountains

Mount Kaya
Mount Ockuyu
Mount Pazar

Elected members are chosen for the intervention of the Emperor's throne

F Zavita: Tall with a strong mind for change aggressive in her expectations

F Azoz: Small framed demure and can be nonresponsive to change

M Intez: A short round stature with no expectations, likes things as they are

M Jyati: Loud and outspoken aggressive with the idea but like things as they are, no consideration to change

M Samar: Tall slender and wants change believes the committee is corrupt and in need of a new body

M Esyr: Mid-body form large and slow tactless in his expectations aggressive with no information to back his ideas

Towns

Menhir
Gwennole
Winog
Ysolda
Quirec

Municipal and federal names of the chosen

- Sadia, f
- Mahed, m
- Hazatt, m
- Kush, m
- Ronett, m

Chapter 11
Spell of Innocence

Day dreams and story books
Are never the same
Seasons go and changes come
As we stand one by one

Cubed in and mesmerised
Asphyxiated again
So it seems in the dream
It's part of the take

Reasons why and alibis
I never can explain
It begins where it ends
Yet isn't to exceed

Always ignoring
What I believe
To live or die a question why, and
What it is to need

Day dreams and story books
I never can explain
To live or die a question why
Or just to watch me bleed

The spell of innocence
is in you now
To dwell on ignorance
Is heaven's hell
The spell of innocence
Is in your soul
You search to find it
In meaning

Sora left the board room and went back to fulfil her duties. For the next few months, everything was routine and she got comfortable with her position the committee members were always unimpressed with everything and constantly complained. It seemed that the earlier she arrived the more they would complain about not having enough time for the mornings. Sora's job was to eavesdrop on the committee members as they readied themselves for the office. And surprisingly, because they were so comfortable, the members talked freely in the halls before meetings or to staff.

The first time Sora heard something was four months after being promoted and the others, working in the estate staff were also hearing different pieces of planning.

"Good morning, Umutt."

"Good morning, Axyan."

As they left their rooms and met in the hall.

The halls of the estate are vast, though because of the design someone can be heard from across the corridor, acoustically it is concert ready at all times.

"Are we ready for the first round?" Umutt asked as they both sauntered towards the embassy offices.

"Yes, we have our five candidates, but, I feel there is discontent within the army. I think they have too much power and if we have an uprising they cannot be defeated," said Axyan entering his area.

"This is very serious and must be brought up at the next meeting," Umutt suggested.

Umutt is not a very confident person and will rely on the majority to make decisions, he finds it easier to provoke decisions by comment or suggestion and leave the rest up to vote by majority. Now that the comment has been made it will be food for thought before the next sit-in.

Axyan acted on the idea immediately and contacted the other three members of the communicator.

"Fanyrottiss here, what can I do for you."

"It's Axyan, I was just with Umutt and brought up something I think we should all be discussing at the next sit-in. I'm referring to the armies, specifically the generals. They want more and are becoming unstable. They could be on the verge of questioning our positions and setting the stage for a coup."

"I have also been feeling the tension from those barbarous simpletons," explained Fanyrottiss.

"This is something we could not combat. Do you not have two generals that are family members by blood and in-laws?" questioned Fanyrottiss.

"Step in and hold a conference with them just to find out how tense the situation is. If there is a way to ease the temperament they would know and be able to help negotiate a deal to ease the frustration and make sure the next election is not disrupted."

"I'll set that up before the next sit-in so we can work out and piece together and negotiate a contract that will satisfy both sides," Axyan said before unlinking himself from communication.

"Yes," said Fanyrottiss. "And I have just the answer. We can play with the Admirals and generals with what they expect to receive from raids after campaigning. We'll continue this at the sit-in. See you then."

"Yes, see you then." And both ended the communication.

* * *

Sit-in One

It was a late start as two of the members arrived an hour after the set time, with no excuse, Fanyrottiss chaired the sit-in, as usual, and Axyan took the minutes. Umutt and Misric took their seats, arriving late, as Fanyrottiss commented "Late as usual," Both gave a sour look of contempt and sat down.

"Now we can go over the minutes of our last meeting and proceed into the order of business," said Fanyrottiss scowling at the tardy duo.

While Axyan read Harour handed out the sit-ins agenda and all began following the minutes. "Upon conclusion, are there any questions or do you feel anything was omitted?" Axyan said looking up at the table's occupants.

Nothing was forwarded so Fanyrottiss took the floor.

"Alright, Old Business, the issue of the admirals and generals has come up again and it is getting tired. There has to be something done to appease them so this is what I am going to suggest, and this will only be in effect until after the next Emperor is elected. When it comes to the campaigns, we will let them keep all that is taken fifty per cent is to be divided between the Admirals and Generals, and the other fifty will be with the soldiers.

"We will omit our tax, twenty-five per cent of it, and let them deal with distribution this will give better time management for planning the next election, and eliminate any confrontation with the armies. All in favour?"

Three hands were raised "all against" Umutrt and Misric raised their hands; the two are the usual objects of discontent.

"Passed," Fanyrottiss announced. "Now onto new business; we are in the search of a new Emperor" the table began to snicker "and we have five new candidates, can the secretary pleased read them out."

Axyan started with what was being whispered in the halls of the estate, "There have been rumours of candidates. Outside of our choice, I have not received any resumes or applications as of late, but it is being suggested that there are three independents that are going to be submitted within the next five months. Therefore, I am imposing that we maintain a small number of two until the applications are received and then decide what to do and how to proceed with this outside involvement of new candidacy. All agreed?"

All the members held up their hands.

"Passed," said Axyan, looking around at the faces before him.

Axyan, giving the book of minutes to Umutt said, "You're up for the minutes today please make them legible so we can have them written out accurately later, thank you."

Umutt looked at him puzzled but, reluctantly, took the duty in any way.

"Now, we have a choice of five names to be reduced to two."

- Sadia, f
- Mahed, mHazatt, mKush, mRonett, m

"These are the chosen five, are there any questions?"

None put any thought to question as this was the only way to keep the table moving and get through the sit-in. There were still five other orders to be addressed but the most important have been discussed and the rest took up the rest of the remaining time.

"The next meeting will be held in two weeks, I would like the histories of all five candidates so we can make a proper decision then we can begin the campaigning and put up a deadline for any other entries. Misric, I would like you to take charge of that responsibility and present it for the next sit-in, thanks. Is there any other business to be presented?" none was entered.

"Then I declare the meeting over and the next to be in two weeks from today, all in favour." All hands were raised "passed," said Axyan and motioned to the food waiting for them against the far wall.

Sit-in Two

Two weeks went by fast and Misric felt pressured even though all the information was kept in one place the room at the "Historical Archives" building the building is vast and finding the histories of each person was very time consuming, for the fat little man. Not only did he have to spend time here but he also had to keep a handle on his own Businesses and make sure the person he left in charge wasn't ripping him off.

Misric is a very distrusting soul, but the reason being is, you can have someone around for years and not really know who they are, come back after a vacation and find everything gone and a new owner with a whole different line of products in place. What do you do then, even as a committee member, who do you go to. Nothing is traceable, and even the new proprietor is innocent and knows nothing other than what they had paid to occupy the store, with a lease for the next year. It happened before, and the only thing to be done was to keep coming back and collect the rent on the lease until the duration. Both parties win, and Misric was able to move back in and resume his business.

The sit-in began with the minutes of the last sit-in. Old business and Misric took the floor.

"He read Sadia's file first. She came from an upper region of Kranaqus on the mountain of Kaya, where she was self-educated, home taught by her parents."

This explains why she is so young in the political arena most home taught children to excel in their studies and has a higher IQ. Being that they have more time and are given more attention to education and studies one on one. It is well documented that the development of these children is at a faster pace than private or public teaching. Of course, the parents have to have a great understanding of curriculum, the money to pay for each year's agenda which, depending on the academics of the grade, could be very expensive.

"Then there are Mahed and Kush, who are from a farming community on the base of the Pazar twins still another small community but with a public school that both attended and went on to the university in that same area. The other two, Mahed and Ronett, are both from the Island and city of Rox both attended the U of Rox and graduated with honours, as did they all. So now we are at the decision-making time and I for one think that we stick to the small towns rather than the hard hitters of the big city. It is much easier to manipulate an innocent mind than someone who might have had a few hard knocks and survived."

Misric suggested while finding his seat, “We have had successes with our decisions in the past, and I assure you the hardliners of the city will be very difficult to direct.” Finding his chair he sat down.

“Well, we have some thinking too, what we need to do is take this information home, look it over, come back for a discussion and bring each candidate to a vote. Out of the five, we need to end up with two, so why don’t we end this sit-in at this point and resume in two weeks after we have read over each file and have a better understanding of the individuals we will vote for the two we want to represent Kranaqus. With that in mind, I move to dismiss all other business and motion to end this sit-in, and resume it two weeks from today, all in favour,” All raised their hands, “all a posed” none rose their hands. “Meeting adjourned” directed Fanyrottiss, “We will see each other in two weeks.

Sit-in Three

After the minutes of the last meeting were read Fanyrottiss took the chair “We have now had time to read the candidates histories can we come to a vote for a decision?” he asked the members.

“No,” said Axyan. “I have some questions to ask each of them and feel that before we can continue I have to know where they stand politically. If we decide that we need to keep this elected leader on longer than the past elected Emperors then we have to know that he/she is going to keep the laws as they are set or have in mind changes to give the people more power over their lives and decisions of votes and law.

Fanyrottiss asked, “Are all in the same mind-set? Can I see a show of hands?”

All were raised except Umutt.

Umutt trying to remain unassuming and in the background has not been successful this time.

And Fanyrottiss asked, “Why have you chosen to stay with me?”

Umutt looked at Fanyrottiss stating, “I felt that there was only the question of speed to find who we want rather than taking our time to choose and missing the usual start of the campaign.”

“Yes, that is a concern, but we do need to find the right person this time, not the easiest manipulated or the most convenient,” exclaimed Fanyrottiss looking around at the members.

“So, this is how it will go the three of you who have chosen to find the right candidate will go and interview the five and bring back your findings so we can make a decision based on where they stand in the view of their office and how easy it will be to keep him/her on the side of the committee or will they take their own direction and propose changes we could never agree on," said Fanyrottiss.

"I move we end this meeting and resume in two weeks to go over your findings, all in favour."

All raised their hands; none opposed.

"We will adjourn and meet again in two weeks."

After the meeting, Harour, Axyan and Misric met outside in the corridor and discussed who is going to meet with whom. Harour took two of the potential candidates and Misric took two more, Ayxan met with the last of the five which was also the furthest, living on the mountain of Kranaqus. Sadia would be the most difficult, because of the distance and her seat holds the smallest per cent of Kranaqus population.

Axyan grabbed a platform and began preparing to leave. He packed clothing for a five-day journey and took off to Kaya Mountain. His travel was uneventful and finding Sadia was easy. It took only a few hours to convince her to take part in the election as one of the candidates with the promise of being Emperor and if not elected to sit as his confidant.

Deception is always a part of the lure to bring in the unsuspecting, and by the time, they understood what they are up against it was always too late. She accepted the invitation and said she would be at the sit-in and await her candidacy.

As they get closer to the beginning of the election the committee gets more and more complacent and indiscriminate, they talk together around whomever without discrimination. This makes eavesdropping easier and suspicion of spying uncertain.

Sora, Aa's and Nehan met Tumi with encouraging updates about the committee members at Sora's layout, that's what is referred to as an apartment, or place of residence, "So, as you know Je-hu has made me the collector, we are to meet here, as often as possible, and put what we know together and I alone will meet with Je-hu. What have you heard?" asked Tumi looking at the three of them intensely.

"Ya," Nehan started in. "I have been talking with the chef while I was prepping dinner and he told me, the committee has already selected their candidates for the election they just need to bring it to a decision of which two are going to run, also, they know that there are three candidates from outside their surveillance and they are a little confused by this. Outside of their decisions, there has never been any one's application to the Emperor's throne except whomever they chose. So there is some suspicion and question as to hidwhy, and how it came about. That's why they've only put in two candidates when usually it's five."

"Also, there is major prep going on in the disposal department, It seems that there is a complete sensitisation before every election and they keep it in order until after the committee has done a thorough inspection," said Raju, looking at Tumi.

"Well, then there is a lot to look into, I expect you to be on your toes and your ears open to anything that is overheard at any time. It seems that there is no discrimination taken and things are being revealed without secrecy or prejudice to whoever is in the room. Be careful and watch your back, it's been suggested that the committee is very paranoid and edgy at election time, their actions may, actually, contradict what's going on," Tumi said, looking at each of them.

Chapter 12
The Archives

They both stood and looked at each other for a few moments and, breaking the icy silence Naveen blurted out “Wow that was a little more intense than I figured it to be. But I got all the subjects, plus two, just in case we didn’t like the first five. I also chose two females just to stir up the decision and maybe find a new directive for the people to consider,” Naveen said proudly while looking at Nayrr intensely just to see his reaction, knowing he was very strong against the idea of women in the political scene.

Nayrr smiled and shook his head, “Well, then, I know your stand on the integration of women in the workforce and entering the political forum. It’s going to take more than an application to turn the interests of the people though. I just hope you’re ready to back her if either of them is chosen.”

‘I am, I think it’s about time we had some real representation for the people and not what has been seen in the past. Especially for the past fifteen years, oppression for children without families and single mothers have been horrifically undermined and that has to change, even single men living on the streets are treated better. They’re given sheltered hostels and food, while the women are left to fend and feed their children on nothing.

The campaigns that take place keeps continuous chaos and disorder in the province, and I think it would all change, with more respect given to the other half, as it has been put, I believe we would see a better understanding of provincial and municipal law. We, females, deserve a voice and it can start with a changed gender with our Emperor, “Naveen explained while manoeuvring from the electricians reach to the door to the escape corridor, and while helping Nayrr as well.” Also, she went on, “it wouldn’t hurt to see a bit of compassion in the government, instead of always having ultimatums, or absolute, because we know where it leads in most cases.”

Nayrr then interjected with “that’s what makes the government, and law, work. When given a decision or judgment for crimes or wrongdoing, ultimatums and punishments are fun and exciting to take part in.” Naveen gave a look of disgust and ignored him through the tunnel for the rest of the walk until they got to Ohn-ohn. Naveen put her hands to her mouth, to stop herself from crying, Nayrr just stood there aghast.

Ohn-ohn was cocooned with red ire’s. They had attacked him while he waited, over the past three days. The thing about red ire’s is they’re vicious predators and can sense a hurt or dying pray from ten kilometres, even underground.

“I should have brought better protection,” exclaimed Naveen.

“Ya, well, we all knew the risks and came anyway, he didn’t die in vain,” Nayrr explained.

They could only watch, knowing what was going on inside the cocoon, as many as fifty, red ire’s, were feasting on Ohn-ohn and if they cut the cocoon they would be next. All they could do is walk away. Finding their way to the entrance, while climbing out, they observed a complement of committee members ready to enter the building.

Sit-in Four

As the committee sat down the minutes of the last meeting were read. After the reading Fanyrottiss took over and went right into what he wanted to know, Harour, What did you find? Harour stood to disclose his discussion with Kush and went on to say

“I confronted Kush and halfway through my proposal he interrupted me and said no. I told him that there would be compensations during the preliminaries but he flat out said no. He gave no explanation and had me directed by security to the back door and put out.”

Giving a bit of a smirk Harour then went onto say “I then went to approach Mahed and he was out of town for at least two weeks so I am still in the process of discovery, thank you.”

“The two you were to look into hold office in town and went to the University of Rox, did they not,” asked Fanyrottiss.

“Yes, they are very well educated on the principles of autocratic policy and the law, so I will follow up on him in the next week.”

“OK, Misric, what about you and your findings?”

"Well, "Hummed Misric "there seems to be a similarity between me and Harour, Hazatt was not at his residence and Ronett has declined to be a part of the candidacy. So as it turns out I am also waiting for the return of my other interview which he is also said to return next week at the same date. So I move that we adjourn this meeting until then. 'All in favour' all hands were raised. 'None opposed' non-did, so two weeks then, let's have some better results."

They all left the board room and went their separate ways.

Sit-in Five

The week went by slowly Misric and Harour met a few times to go over how they presented themselves during the first few interviewees and felt it was in the presentation as to why they got a negative response from both ministers. So they worked together to find the best way to present their proposal because the committee wants at least two commitments from the selected candidates.

As Misric readied himself for the trip to the Pazar Twins he turned on the communicator and called Harorur, "I just want to go over how I am to confront Hazatt one more time. I don't want to embarrass myself at the next sit-in and if we can get both to participate it would make for better performance on our side and a greater possibility to win the Emperor's seat."

"OK," said Harour, and they spent the greater part of the day addressing the questions and the introduction to them. When Misric was satisfied, and a little more secure with himself they ended the communication and Misric finished putting together his travelling supplies. When they talk about weeks they mean nine days, it takes five days to make the journey there and back leaving two days of interview and decision.

Misric left the next day.

Harour met with Mahed the following week and it took some major convincing but he agreed to go to the first sit-in before the running dates, just in time and there is just four more days before the fifth sit-in and he hasn't heard from Misric yet.

As they began getting settled for the fifth sit-in Fanayrottis addressed the committee, "Before we begin the meeting I have hard news to tell all of you, Misric is dead."

They all gasped.

“It’s not clear how it happened but there is some speculation of an ambush, and foul play. As it also turns out he did not make his meeting with his second interviewee, Hazatt. So Fanyrottiss appointed Axyan to go persuade Hazatt to join the Emperor race for election. And the fifth sit-in was adjourned.”

Chapter 13

Misric was on his way to Ysolda. He had packed enough for the five-day excursion plus a few extras in case he needed or wanted to stay a few extra days. His first two days were without incident and he began to relax, thinking that there was nothing but the interview to look forward to, so he began going over how he is going to conduct it when he got there. Levitating over the open sand dunes, central to this region he noticed what looked like the beginning of a campaign on the desert population.

There were no scheduled targets, due to the election, in the next few months. All focus is to maintain peace to focus and support the coming campaign promotion of the next Emperor. So he decided to go down and have a look at the action, when it was over he approached the general and asked, "What is your company?"

Misric demanded looking over the battlefield and observing how many had been killed.

"General Ishan, company one six, I have been given orders to subdue this region for unpaid taxes and treason. We, several leaders, taken into custody. And ask your permission to carry on," General Ishan asked saluting.

Misric was astonished, at his request and his expectation to do so without question.

Misric's reply surprised Ishan. "Who ordered this?"

"Admiral Kuchunji."

"You know that a campaign like this must go through the procedure and be voted on by the comity, this is an act of civil insubordination and is punishable by loss of rank or death. We are in the beginnings of an election and actions like this can severely hurt any cooperation by the people and bring in the wrong majority."

"We have no political agenda and do not care what the committee has as theirs. We are only interested in the law and taxation is what we have been sent to balance here at this time." Glaring at Misric and holding his sheathed sabre as a threat.

"Well, we have had our sit-ins and have had extensive reports on the balances and deficits of each region and this area is not and has not ever been on any of the reports as an arrear or a questionable contempt of payment," Misric answered, with as much unyielding observance.

"That's as much as he remembers when regained consciousness, he tried to speak but nothing happened it was like he is paralysed. Misric could see his feet and there is nothing binding him, all he could do is listen and observe what was going on around him, and it didn't seem good. The General and his men were talking about how easy it was to capture the unsuspecting fool. Fanayrottis was right this idiot was always too curious to a fault, and how, it is his last time to interfere with plans made for the future.

"Keep digging," said Ishan."

"We have to be finished with this by nightfall there is more to be readied in Rox, the campaign starts in a few weeks and things must be perfect," he continued as he strutted about his men.

Misric could see there were only a few, maybe six or seven. Thinking to himself.

"I hope they're not talking about me if they are, when I get out of this there will be hell to pay" He tried moving again but nothing was responding it was as if he has been a victim of the blown powder the comity is so apt to using on unwanted ministers, guests, or political rivals that the people show a strong interest in and may defeat the candidate they want on the Emperor's seat.

"Go in and get the insubordinate" the general directed, that's when Misric realised it is him there referring to and he might not be getting out of this too soon. Just at that moment three soldiers grabbed him and his platform and took him outside. Placing him in front of the hole the general stepped forward and began with.

"Personally, I have nothing against you, but I have been given specific orders and you are to be executed," looking around at the dunes and the area he had chosen, as desolate as it is, the oasis in the middle of nowhere is the most appropriate place he could find given the circumstances and the unexplained reasons "I don't know why this is being done to you, but there is a value to every loss and gain in this life and you have a great value to me at this time, if I could spare you I would but in the end, everything is known and then I would be on the chopping block, so it's better you then me. If you have a god or a deity to pray to do it now you have fifteen minutes to do so before I return." General Ishan turned to his accompanying crew of soldiers and said, "Let us leave him to contemplate his last minutes and we will return in fifteen, dismissed."

Misric watched them all leave, where to, he didn't know, they just disappeared and he was alone, "*Fanyrottiss, you ire, YOU RED IRE,*" he thought to himself "*I knew there was something up with you when you gave me this assignment,*" because of the impairment of the blowing dust, there was nothing he could do but wait, wait for his final outcome and inevitable death. Just then two figures came dropping down from above.

"Well, I guess you didn't expect to be rescued," Misric just stared in amazement, Naveen and Nayrr busily worked together putting him on his platform and, Nayrr attaching him to a tether, began towing him towards the open dunes. "Though it is an exposed open expanse," Nayrr said, "The soldiers will not see us. The oasis causes a humid like mirrored haze that camouflages everything after a half-, and we'll be much further than that in less time than it takes to make a peanut butter sandwich."

One of the soldiers came running back to General Ishan "He's gone."

"What do you mean, he's gone," replied Ishan.

"I went to see how he was and he isn't there," the soldier said excitedly.

"That's impossible," replied Ishan. "There is no way he could have escaped, the dust would not have worn off and we are the only ones in the area, how could this happen," General Ishan questioned as he walked back to observe. Finding it to be true he ordered everyone to fan out to find the renegade. They looked for hours and found nothing. And all Ishan could do was look stunned and confused.

So he ordered the six remaining soldiers who remained behind to do this act of treachery to line up, readying themselves to return to Rox. The general was strangely standing farther away than usual, but before they could question what was on, a stomper pummelled them to the ground.

General Ishan then busied himself to put the bodies onto the dug grave, meant for Misric, burying them and making sure the sight could never be found.

Generals – 25 Regiments

(1) Byman, (2) Soe, (3) Achily, (4) Broj, (5) Endah, (6) Vuyll, (7) Saad, (8) Babol, (9) Lohar, (10) Zio, (11) Javu, (12) Sai, (13) Mahya, (14) Datu, (15) Axillyaz, (16) Ishan, (17) Lothya, (18) Adas, (19) Yoaranett, (20) Juvaya, (21) Himoro, (22) Atula (23) Zam, (24) Kaz and (25) Syaas.

Their weaponry and armament are of Sparta, as well as roman war tech.

Silo: Armament, weapons and…

Berserker: Front line and rear flanking strategy of attack.

Admirals – 5

1. Intaz: A large insightful operative with an aggressive attitude
2. Mohid: Well-rounded diplomatic and narrow-minded
3. Raju: Tall muscular lacks diplomacy is aggressive ready to fight without purpose
4. Rois: Insightful and aggressive diplomatic yet ready to battle if he doesn't hear what he wants or there is no compromise between parties
5. Kuchunji: Aggressive always ready to battle non-diplomatic a large muscular tactless individual with no couth.

Admirals: genuinely ridged with a narrow-minded focus, loyalty is expected with a winning outcome to every campaign.

Chapter 14
This Day of Question
Communications to Devi Log Entry

I have been travelling through forested areas for the past five weeks and my psoriasis has been the worst it ever was on my home planet. I believe it's because of the humid air and funguses in the forests but there is no way to battle this as my salve has been used a few weeks before. In my travels, though, I wandered into a small village seeking shelter, supplies and a possible remedy for my scaling head. While observing my dilemma and torment they offered a sour juice something like vinegar on our world but these Quaians called it cider.

It was in the form of many applications one a shampoo, a bathing liquid, a soapy gel and a tonic for external and internal gestation. While I bathed I would apply it to my scalp and let it sit for twenty minutes. After rinsing apply the bathing liquid, rinse again, towel dry and let it do its work. A few days later it would be gone.

I don't mean partially, it was completely gone. Relieved I took enough to continue using just in case of another outbreak. As I completed my journey, and to also duplicate, the seeds I've stored, so I could bring them back to my home planet.

On my planet, we have been suffering from this problem for centuries with no finding of a cure and as we get older it tends to get worse. Apples are not grown on Devi Any longer. They have been extinct for a century from a disease caused by a tic that would lay its eggs into the fruit and after the larvae change, it left the pupa behind which created a fungus. Quickly spreading over a period of fifty rotations it eliminated that resource, killing the tic but as well, causing the extinction of apples.

I felt not only relief but an opportunity for myself, relief for my world and a fortune in the making. I began to grin with such fever that my face started to cramp and tick at the same time. The people of this village believe in this stuff so much that they bathe in it at least once or twice a month. They say it keeps the fungus at bay and refreshes their spirit. It does have refreshing scent and keeps the scaling completely away so the benefits aren't without merit.

All for now, Je-hu

The Path

I am but a ghost
On the path
To seek light
The light
Is with you both
Be it wrong
Or be it right

My thoughts
My dreams
A plot
Or a theme
Are leading me
Through each night

Atten, Devi committee members

Because there have been so many questions and reasons between the committee members about what and why we have made the choices we are engaging now, all you should have are patients and admiration for my team. Losing the battle is not an option. I can only accept the decision from Devi as an important part of the work but make my own decisions based on my knowledge and interaction with the people of Qua. It seems the longer I am here the farther away Devi becomes. And, though we can communicate periodically the day to day here makes the decisions, by me that much more frustrating yet encouraging, the distance is always going to be a major factor.

I don't know what to expect but the content is important. So I will just do what I have to do and wait, but at the same time, not stagnate. It is very disturbing that the committee of Kranaqus think they can use this time to make everything go in their favour. To work it out is in our best interest to remain secret and so there, for me, is doubt. Whatever the outcome only time can tell but for now, it's planning and communication. With the board on Devi, they need to be patient I can only act on what I know, and I believe I have the right consideration for the position.

All I know is this energy and the time shared, even the bad, is growth and it turns out to be true. Even bad times are better than nothing at all.

Je-hu's final correspondence with, the committee of Devi.

Je-Hu

The next communication is to a lost love that Je-hu cherished and, after this letter was never returned with a response, found himself angry and without hope of saving.

When I see your smile, I don't know if my team did this to me on purpose or if it's their way of reminding me, there is a rapport I need to remain attentive to. They made me aware of the interpersonal scope that is shared between two who are united. So I thought I would send you this correspondence.

I hope things aren't as troubling there as they are for me here, as you are always in it. Troubling circumstances, I mean. And what I want to say is here is what I see. When I look at you and we're quiet, what I see troubles me.

These things you don't see. In your chaos, you are much organised, and it keeps a handle on your work, when you're at it, it's how you know each square. With each given day you find a new beginning you make life worth living and I can't throw a good thing away. Sometimes, when a word rhymes, when the sun shines, when the birds have all left the trees, the way it's always had something to do even though you might be making it up.

You have a great imagination and if you would sit down and really put your mind to writing, even a short story, you would find where your strengths lay. Write to its conclusion you'll be that much closer to seeing what I know is in you. These are just some things, I'll write to you more each time, OK.

When

When I look at you
All I see is forever
When I see you smile
The full moon starts rising
And there isn't anyone
To say this to
And I know
I'd rather be with you

So
I ask myself
if it's me
I've deceived
As I hide behind
This rendering pen
And find another place
To be perceived

When I see a new
That time is
In the air
And the world I see
Isn't forgotten
And that I'd rather
Be seeing you
And there's no one
To say this to

When I look
At you
My mind is aloof
When I feel
A new
The world gets better
The wat it's
Meant to be
When I'm with you

The character that came out while we were together is what you need to achieve your goal, your enthusiasm will show in the pursuit and in the doing. To accomplish this you must pull out that character. The plan is already there all you have to do is put it together.

Patients: A great quality you possess

Giving: A great virtue and one that draws people to you

Informed: So you can advise without being pretentious

Caring: Clients will know that you will take the time and effort to give them your best

Love always and forever, Je-hu

* * *

This next correspondence is with a citizen whom he has befriended and thought it would lead to a relationship but she made a wrong move that put her into a very disturbing circumstance and Je-hu lost touch after these correspondences.

Hello Je-hu

My day is very boring over here in "Dakar Senegal Prison". In this camp, we find it hard to go out because we are not allowed to do so. Staying in the prison l hope l will get out of this soon. I don't have any relatives now that I can go to.

All my relatives ran away in the middle of the war. The only person I have now is Rev. Joseph Udel, who is the Reverend Pastor of the prison. In the camp, he has been very good to me since l came to this place, but meanwhile, I am not living with him, rather, I'm living in the women's hostel.

The camp has two hostels one for men the other for women. The Pastor, when you send correspondence, goes to him to be delivered to the inmates. As a refugee, I don't have any right or privilege to anything pertaining to money or whatever is classified as personal belongings because it is against the law while imprisoned in this country. I want to go back to my studies because I only attended my first year before the tragic incident that leads to my being in this situation. I look forward to any correspondence from you, it is the only thing I have that takes me away from this solitude.

Sincerely,
Ishan

Reading this correspondence from Ishan, while visiting friends, found herself caught in the middle of a coup. Je-hu amuses himself with these letters, citizens he has befriended from home, just to pass the time. Knowing he cannot involve himself with their issues he collects them and makes them a part of his journal, a response from Je-hu after receiving the letter from Ishan.

My friend Ishan,

So, it's begun! I wasn't going to mention it but let you find out for yourself. You put yourself thereafter I warned you about the ferocity of the government. But you get what it is you need when you don't heed the warnings. Here it is then, it won't seem like it at first and it may not be a conscious thing so don't question them on it, just be aware.

Subconsciously there is a conspiracy to prevent you from your goal of education. It starts subtly but eventually becomes overwhelming with your time expectancy, taking you out, demanding frivolous things to be done, as it was last night, which is why I knew not question your whereabouts. Anger is what you have to be expecting when you try to approach them on it trying to call the shots. This is just the beginning of it. That's why I'm trying to find you some resources on my end.

I don't know why the prison is so reluctant to give out information; you would think they would want intelligent people of their refugees but apparently not. It is only reserved for citizens, though they say education is an open door. You will begin to notice, as registration day draws closer and you start to irritate them with any conversation of it. Especially the Reverend and other inmates, in some weird way they are working together. I just thought you should know.

There are a few more things but that can wait. Just be aware that there is a thoughtlessness about what they think you are capable of achieving.

You are in my thoughts and I hear you, your friend always, Je-hu.

The response from Ishan.

Dear Je-hu,

I am writing this mail to you with heavy tears in my eyes and great sorrow in my heart. I am contacting you because I don't have any other option than to tell. I am now married to Toyo who worked with the embassy in Burkina for nine years before we married. After an explosion in the mine, he took a leave of absence.

They were married for eleven years without a child and after a brief illness that lasted for only five days, she died. When she was alive he deposited the sum of USD 8.2m in a bank in Ouagadougou the capital city of Burkina.

Presently this money is still in the bank. He made this money available for the exportation of Gold from Burkina mining. Recently, My Doctor told me that I would not last for a period of seven months due to a cancer problem. The one that disturbs me most is my stroke sickness.

Having known my condition I decided to hand you over this money to take care of the less-privileged people. You will utilise this money the way I am going to instruct herein. I want you to take thirty per cent of the total money for your personal use while seventy per cent of the money will go to charity: people in the street and helping any orphanage.

I grew up as an Orphan, and I don't have any family members to pass the money onto. As soon as I receive your reply, I shall give you the contact of the bank in Burkina and I will also instruct my lawyer to issue you an authority letter that will prove you the present beneficiary of the money. That is if you assure me that you will act accordingly as I Stated herein.

Hoping to receive your reply.

Sincerely,
Ishan

Je-hu could not accept the responsibility of this, while he is involved with the light streamers and jumping in and out of other worlds. He was humoured by the gesture and reads the letters to reassure himself that what he is doing is right and that the field of the Web will give the citizens of Devi the opportunity to continue their quests of entitlement and pursue their objectives in life and love.

Chapter 15
It Begins

The beginning of the election, to find a new Emperor, is in eighteen months that's just enough time to find a candidate and put together a campaign, to run against the committee.

Axyan, thought to himself, "*What is the purpose of sending me, Fanyrottiss has nothing better to do with himself and I've already brought in one potential. I think he should show his expertise and interview this newt.*"

As he put together a touring bag, "*of course I'm not going to oppose this decision I know where that would get me, and that is not what I intend to have happened,*" he went on thinking aloud "*Misric and Umutt are already facing the discipline and then there were three,*" he thought to himself, as he plugged in his platform to be charged. He started to open a communication with Fanyrottiss but what would he say, or rather complain about and thought better of it.

He planned to leave the next day, so he took some time, a little self-time, and sent out for some intimate indulgence. Communications are private so the discovery of calls can only be disclosed by archive storage libraries. If Fanay were to get word of my appetites I'm sure I would be taken for the next disappearance. The males were of his taste, as he enjoys eating some of the most exotic of creations. After a night of sex and debauchery, Axyan was ready to proceed. He hopped onto his platform and was off.

He will be gone for five days at least or longer if he has to be persuasive. The region he has to pass through it can be quite dangerous. Yosalda dwells on the outside of the Pazar Twins, to get there can be very precarious. There are several things to watch out for, one being the creatures that fly.

There are small insects that can imbed themselves into the surface of the skin and take over your whole bloodstream with their larvae. Mostly they attack from behind where it is hard to fend them off, and the only way to fight them is to wear a mesh cape garment that these parasites cannot penetrate. They are known as Xyxus, they are found in very few areas, and have many enemies. All kinds of creatures seek out these vermin as a staple, and because they are regional and territorial they are easy to find in hatching season.

They are seasonal and predictable so they have a limited time to reproduce and to find hostess to inoculate. During the hibernation, of the animal, the eggs spread throughout the bloodstream and become parasites that attach themselves to the inner lining of the artery walls and overwhelm the host while sleeping. But when it enters the seasonal host it, as the parasites take over, causes the host to become lethargic, by giving off venom that slows the metabolism and puts the host into a deep simulated sleep. They can then devour their victim as they continue to chrysalis and become the flying predators they are.

Because the hosts are always migrants, it is hard to know where they will be, at any given season, but it is not usually outside the lower Kaya and Pazar twins forests, because the forests meet at various parts of the region.

Axyan, chose to travel through the desert, it avoids these types of predators being so dry and it shortens the trip by three days. The next day he set out, getting to his platform was a chore he didn't want to leave knowing the dangers but they were easier to face than Fanay, at least there is protection from those. Starting he'll go around Ockuyu, the typical route is the safest, and then a hard left through the desert.

It's a good thing there are taverns along with the ways he can gather enough water to make the journey as durable as he can, *"It can be done in two and a half days on one of these things.*" He thought to himself. Getting to the desert's edge was uninterrupted and actually relaxing. He found a tavern about a mile from the desert's threshold and booked a room.

The next morning he crossed into the desert region and the heat hit him like a brick hitting a glass sheet, shattering into beads of perspiration. In the first few hours, he drank two quarts of fluids and realised that if he kept up that kind of consumption he'll finish his reserve in one day so he began to ration and plan for the two days of travel. Crossing into the dunes took half a day, the first part of the dunes are flat, the turbulent air storms and winds is what causes the dunes and they are always shifting.

"This form of travel is the best way to avoid the trappings of the sands and its creature inhabitants. So the only thing I'll be battling in the heat, that is until I get into the forests of Pazar." Axyan thought aloud. The two days of travelling the dunes were unremitting and the heat made it almost unbearable but when he saw the forest edge, on the third day, and mountain peaks behind them he was reassured that there was life at the end of this desolation.

Because he hadn't travelled much on Qua, the thing he didn't realise is, predators are everywhere. His travel experience has been throughout Rox and nothing farther than mount. Ockuyu. This region is where Zyus and Dracos are found. They are lower land beasts.

And, even though they are winged beasts, their metabolism does not allow them to fly more than 1,500 feet above sea level. Except on rare occasions offspring can, but, only if they are born at higher elevations, still, they are apt to dwell and bread, in the lower regions, due to the size and resource of prey. In the higher elevations, food is scarce, and the air is thin.

Axyan starts getting eager seeing the view of the forest in the foreground but doesn't notice the black-winged creatures soaring above the trees, and that's where he had in mind to travel. The winged creatures spread out, as they are harder to spot when going in for the grab or kill. Axyan is levitating three metres above the sand and begins to climb to be above the trees. It will be a less obstructed route to Ysolda, so he thinks.

As he entered the tree line, soaring above it, he failed to observe the dark figures separating and doing a one-eighty, in order to overtake their subject from behind. The mother of the two offspring is showing them how to ambush her intended victim. She swoops in from behind Axyan and surprises him, but, as she goes for the grab with her huge talons, a gust of wind throws Axyan off balance and he falls to his knees onto the flat board.

"Holy shit, that Ire bitch Zyu, almost got me," he said allowed, he then ducked below the treetops and into the cover of the forest, a more hazardous flight but a harder view for the Zyu. Now he has to slow down in order to avoid being struck or skewered by a branch or a hidden obstacle.

From one hazard to another, *"I hope this is the worst of it I don't need any more surprises,"* he thought to himself, trying to focus on what is in front of him as well as the dark figures above him. The trees made it hard to negotiate but it would be just as troubling for the Zyu.

"Thought I was easy prey, Hugh!" shaking his fist at the Zyu he crouched down lowering the platform to a more grounded level, he found it easier to control and the trees easier to manoeuvre around. Although his speed is reduced he seems to still be making good time.

"Wow, I hope this speed can be kept up," as he looked around at the density of the tree growth. "This could easily consume me and no one would ever know I was here, I'd best be diligent on my path so as not to be slammed into oblivion." The rest of the trip was uncompromising by hazards or creatures, although he did see some big suspicious-looking animals, over the next few hours, before coming to the district he was looking for.

Searching for the area where he will find Hazatt, the district he holds office is just outside the small township in the farming community. This is divided up into three districts. You wouldn't think that there were a big population in the farming sector, but citizens farm to make themselves relied upon, and to maintain a low profile. Landowners can only own what they can maintain on an annual basis, of course, the plots are double size so fields can be alternated every three years, to prevent overuse and keep the soil rich.

Hazatt holds office in district two, but resides in town, he would be in his office right now but, Axyan wanted to wait, and settle into a room at the nearby tavern. He can then look up the residence of Hazatt and go over unannounced, in the late hours. In the meantime, he decided to get some needed rest.

He awoke, startled by a commotion outside his room, getting up to look he found it was nothing crucial. Realising the time he began getting prepared to go see Hazatt. The thing about PMs (persons of ministries), they are not difficult to find. Hazatt's office is in his residence so it wasn't a challenging endeavour.

As Axyan approached two dogs met him at the fence Axyan froze. Looking to the left he noticed a communication device and buzzed it, a face appeared on the screen, "Hello, can I help you?"

Axyan then answered, "Yes, I'm from the municipality of Rox and a representative of the committee. I have a proposition for you and need to converse with you for a few hours, if you can make the time now that would be fantastic. I can come back tomorrow but now is the better time. I have to return to Rox ASAP."

Hazatt answered, "I am actually busy until next week can it wait until then."

. "No," Axyan replied.

"OK, I have a full day tomorrow but can make time at mid-day for a couple of hours, is that good for you?" Hazatt asked.

"Yes, that will be great, I'll see you then, Good day."

Axyan then went back to his place of accommodation and ordered the late-day meal. Early the next day he started to prepare himself for the mid day's meeting, including the early meal, preparation took up most of the time. He then went to Hazatts residence to go through the interview. Axyan noticed, as he arrived, the dogs were not on the grounds.

Hazatt told him to come right in through the front entrance and directed Axyan towards the living quarters. Motioning him to sit, he asked, "What are you here to sell, if you don't mind my frankness?"

"Not at all." Axyan gestured and continued, "I'll be just as blunt with why I'm here."

So Axyan went through the proposal which took an hour and ended with "the committee will not take no for an answer, and expect you there for the preparations and groundwork. The running begins in fifteen weeks. We will send an escort to bring you to the Sit-in before it's in session."

Hazatt just sat there and looked at him for a few moments before saying, "I guess there is no refusing this honour."

"No, there will be consequences if you do," Axyan said looking at him sternly.

"Well, then, it appears that I have some time to put my business in order to prepare for an election that I am to be rewarded with great honour. Or, be defeated by unknown rivals, as they… you have suggested. Not making them known is a frustration, and now, though I am only registered in unwillingness," Hazatt said looking back with abated Indifference.

"I'll see you at the time you have stated and will be ready for whatever the decision is when we go through the process of votes."

They both stood and shook hands. Hazatt walked his uninvited guest to the door and after Axyan left, he went back to the living area to contemplate what he had just been approached with.

Axyan exited the residence went to his board and back to the quarters he is staying at and prepared to leave. While he was doing so he got a hold of Fanyrottiss, on the communicator.

"I have just seen Hazatt and gave him no alternative but to come to the preliminaries and be a part of the program, joining the election to become Emperor."

"Excellent," replied Fanyrottiss.

Chapter 16
The Campaign

The government of Zed Knows the power of Akir, and that they are weak. Except for the fact that their alliance with Kranaqus makes them a force they can only hope to hold off. Zed, back from the attack, can, maybe, just hold a position on the land they occupy. With the minimal support Akir gets from Kranaqus, leadership is befuddled.

The difficulty is to attack with the intent of occupying the land as a whole. Every town and village have their own government set its own rules and laws of direction, yet with Kranaqus structure of direction is an achieved embodiment.

After being attacked by Akir and having their weaponry destroyed by them, they have again rearmed themselves with laser weaponry and are going to use it to defeat, and overrun the province of Akir. Akir has no Idea what they have planned and will not expect this raid on the lower province. So Zed gathers their armies to get ready for the first confrontation with Akir. What they don't know is Akir has received information on Zeds interests and know about their intent.

With their alliance, Kranaqus has promised that they will be protected from any and all outside campaigning with Zed. Having set up reinforcements to stop zed from crossing into Akir, Akir was waiting, Undisclosed to Zed, with stompers. Zed had reinforced their army with more than one hundred lasers, and with some innovations. Handheld, compact laser rifles, will make taking out these weapons difficult.

Though few lasers were on the field, twenty-five handheld were all they felt necessary, and thirteen stationary, on mobile mounts. The stompers had to be pre-set and they are not stationary positions. So they have to think of an alternative solution.

Using stompers, Akir set them at the front, because they are so new they have only two settings. Quick to manoeuvre they can only be used as front-line assault, with the left to right, or forward and reverse. Knowing where the laser aggressors are was very important, so they could be pinpointed and eliminated before they did too much damage. They have only five stompers for use at this time, they are air levitation devices.

Needed is someone on high ground in order to see where the handheld and mobile lasers are coming from or the stompers would be useless.

General Juvaya owed the committee a favour and therefore was sent to help Akir to fend off the Zed from their attack. He was given use of five stompers and ten others as backup, as they only have fifty ready to use. Stompers are difficult to make and, if destroyed, are hard to replace. And that is exactly what happened, during the assault on Akir three stompers were taken out immediately by Zed's mobile lasers.

With only two left, the General, set them at a low altitude so he could get the maximum effect. He widened the radius of the beam and took out two mobiles along with, about twenty-five soldiers, one with a handheld laser rifle. His focus was then on the laser's positions now, and they were not going to be easy.

The soldiers he had, manipulating the stompers, were ordered to concentrate on the laser's rifles, but before doing so, taking out the remaining mobile would be necessary. Because of the size of the guns on the mobile beasts, they were slow and clumsy so taking it out was fast and easy. The soldiers using the rifles, for some reason though, being stationary was the best use of operation.

So the General took advantage of their mistake and stomped two more out, but not before they evaporated many more of the ground troops, some in his own regiment. Now there are only two high tech weapons, on each side, and General Juvaya lowered the stompers to ground level until he saw where the rifle lasers were, just when a beam hit a group rushing into the Zed front line. One of the stompers was right in front of the soldier who fired it, and he quickly responded taking out several surrounding soldiers as well.

Seeing their losses, and knowing they only have three lasers left online, Zed decided it would be a good time to retreat, and did so without haste. Regrouping in the fortress they resupplied themselves with armament and reinforcement of soldiers.

"We have to take out the last remaining stomper or we are lost," said the Zed general.

"There are more tech weapons we didn't use and, different devices found on the field. They will be a part of the reinforcement and recovery unites," he pointed at the group that was entering the armoury just then.

They had the weapons at hand and looked eager.

Outside the gates of the fortress, Akir and their allies were regrouping and making ready for a defence attack. Because they had lost all but one, of their stompers, more were sent to the front. Stompers have a very high speed and can travel vast distances in minutes rather than hours or days. The maximum speed has not been determined, it has never been tested, and this is the first time it has been used in battle.

Stompers are not impenetrable, but they replace many different weapons and can be used in place of soldiers, saving many from senseless or premature death. They were thought to be used as a flanking resource but have proven to be front line aggression as well, so far as proven in this field of battle.

Setting their camp as far back from the field Akir began to make camp. The boundaries are set behind the grass blades. They grow fast and will act as a defence against any who try to overtake them during the eclipse. They are not rare but are periodic, happening as often as four times in succession depending on the alignment of the planets.

The alignment that is happening now takes place every five orbits, it is not the same each time and cannot be predicted. But, when it happens, depending on the size of the planet and the order they fall each eclipse can last days. Although there are four suns they do not always face each planet at all times.

When the smaller planets move in front of Qua they can be in complete darkness, depending on where the orbit is and the suns are faced. Right now the suns are at the farthest point of Qua putting each smaller planet is in almost total darkness when passing Qua. Qua has a haze of light, as the fourth sun is sitting low on the horizon and as each planet passes Qua the shadow caused by the planet creates a darkness that is terrifying to most of the citizens.

The first of the planets has started its pass and darkness blankets Akir and the battleground like a dome that has been placed over the region encasing it in isolation. It is one of the larger planets so it is expected to last at least a week. The next is the central planet, one day, the next large planet one week and the last five days. This will cause a rift in the battle dragging into possibly weeks or a month, depending on the planning and execution of each engagement.

The first planet was just beginning to make its appearance on the region and the wind, blowing from the north felt oddly cold.

"We have the dark on our side, it crests on the mountains, I would like to send out teams of reconnaissance for the first two dark periods."

Periods are used, instead of night, that way it distinguishes the light from the dark. They don't refer to the dark times as night because it isn't separated consistently to give equal time measurement or certainty.

"This way we can get an idea of what we're dealing with how many of those huge devices we face, and where they are. Then in the third period, we can send a team to attack in stealth. You all know how difficult it is in the dark but again, it can advantage us and give us the edge and send them back with their tails between their legs and, maybe hold some ground this time." the captain grunted. "I'll need volunteers, four. Come see me in an hour when you've reached a decision."

The first team made their entrance, each team is made up of four volunteers, "I want two teams sent out flanking the right and left of their camp. It will be dark at least a week and we want to take total advantage of this time." The commander explained.

The Akir is only fighting, in alliance with to Kranaqus, to maintain their interests of peace. Akir is a peaceful province and does not seek aggression. It is the interests of Kranaqus that makes this happen. Akir must supply citizens during periods of campaigning.

And, what the Zed does not want is Kranaqus to convert Zed into a state under them. So Zed must position themselves in Akir with the objective of taking over. In this way, they will maintain their freedoms and form an alliance with Akir.

The teams, when they did not return, were thought to be captured or lost. It has been two dark periods with no report or return and with only six periods remaining, Zed has to act with speed. It takes nine periods, or days, for the planet Fauiq to pass.

"We must create a new plan," the captain stated, glancing at his next two teams.

The temperature takes such an extreme change when the planets are so close and their shadows, during this time, are so dark. The orbit of this solar system is erratic, because of the gravitational pull of the four suns, the planets change the direction of rotation every year. Every five years of a seven-year pattern, there is a sequential alignment of the planets as they pass Qua. The order differs in some way each time as well as the placement of the shadows.

This affects the atmosphere causing extreme overcast and negative temperatures.

Everything is affected and activities are dictated by the shadows' movement over the planet. Planning for such change is important; it becomes a matter of life or death. Whole villages are lost due to poor planning.

Of the five planets, Qua is the largest. The orbit of each planet is skewed due to the drift of the solar system and gravitation of the suns and can, at times, cause the planets to be in a very close alignment with Qua. This casts a shadow on both surfaces where the temperatures, on the smaller planet can fall to degrees in the minus Celsius. As Qua is the largest planet its shadow is the first to be encountered causing the beginning of cooling, with smaller planet, the temperatures, by the time Qua aligns with the planets orbit the planet's temperature can be in the minus degrees which causes a flash freeze on Qua, as it rotates. With the shadow on its surface Qua it reflects the temperature of the smaller planet. The planet moves in sync with the rotation of Qua fixing the darkness in one region, along its surface lowering temperatures to negative degrees on both planets.

In the shadows centre temperatures can reach minus twenty-seven Celsius, and on the inner topographic point, temperatures can range between plus five and negative five, depending on the orbit. Suns are skewed and displaced and can be offset exposing the planets to the inner universe which leads to colder temperatures.

Upon this crossing Zed and Akir are in shadow with Fauiq. It will not end until the planets are passed and Qua is completely facing the sun again. The next to cross is Devi. Its shadow takes twelve days to complete and will land on the desert and plains of Kranaqus, but it has less effect on the region due to a more dispersed shadow allowing more light and stronger temperatures in the plus.

Serxho is next to pass followed by Ekrem. Their shadows will land on the opposite side of Qua. In the water regions, Serxho will touch Qua during its pass dropping temperatures to below zero, but it is on the edge of the shadow allowing for some light and heat from the sun. As the planets pass the largest planet, the rotation begins to be acted on.

As the shadow from the smaller planet begins to appear on Qua clouds start to accumulate and it begins to snow as the planets begin a gradual slowing on their axis. Land quakes are natural as this happens, storms as well, in these shadows it will snow. During these times little can happen. Campaigns do go on because there are preparations made.

Advance warnings and signs, with wildlife as well as astronomical observation, gives enough information to ready themselves for the cold.

At the fort the Zed captain stood on the turret with his lieutenant, looking into the distance, observing the lights from the Akir camp.

"We can surprise them." the lieutenant implied.

"How, look at the brilliance of their camp. We couldn't get within ten kilometres undiscovered," the captain said with disdain. The lieutenant looked at him and reminded him, "Some of our men are Akirians, they can easily disguise themselves and set up an ambush, all we want is one prisoner."

"We should have thought of that on the battlefield, before picking, we should have fingered one of them, preferably a top aide."

"We need some intelligence," said the captain.

"But how," he mumbled.

"We have six periods left, we need to find the Akir strengths to know, without knowing we have less opportunity, what we have in our arsenal is going to sustain us until the next attack. The darkness does not show mercy when you get stuck in the cold it takes a hold of your will to go forward." Just at that moment, the Lieutenant got a brilliant idea.

"How many handheld laser rifles do we have?"

"That is… an unknown. I had some of the recruits go over the field, as the first stages of the shadow began, to gather as many handhelds as they could find. It seemed that the Akir and Kranaqus had an endless supply. So, I ordered a search for anything that worked and even then smashed or nonworking they could be used for research.

"Also, by swapping parts we could fix some for reuse. I know that some of the deserters from Akir we have on-staff have worked in the Kranaqus labs and have used and worked with technology… I've got them on it now, I can go down and see how many we have for use.

"Good, go now and count how many we have. Test the working devices for distance. These things are light-streak firing devices, it must be able to travel some distance before burning out. Accuracy, distance and volatile power are what we're looking for." he advised the lieutenant.

"Yes sir," he saluted. As he left the room the captain reiterated, "Distance, that is the priority."

"Distance." the lieutenant repeated.

Walking in on the technician the lieutenant asked, "What have you discovered?"

"Well, there is a major muddle of piecing things together and separating parts, when these things burn out the central core fuses. Meaning, it becomes useless and needs to be replaced, completely. This means, though it can be removed we have no replacement core. And the gun is rendered unusable.

"But not all these devices are damaged and are interchangeable. I have also discovered a psychological feature or level of attitude, in other words, a low setting and a high setting. This I have yet to test. I've been waiting for your advice on how to proceed. Do you want me to do some experimentation or just ready them to be used?" the tech asked.

"I want to know what the range of these devices is and their capabilities, strengths from the lowest setting to powers of mid and max settings. Grab two of these weapons and let's go out to the courtyard for a firing experiment," the lieutenant said.

As they walked out to the courtyard the tech turned to the lieutenant realising, "We can't do this here."

"Why?"

"We're going for distance… so the area would be an asset. Which means the courtyard is too small. I would suggest that we go to the outer boundary and into the forest. We'll need to be in a place high off the ground like the cliffs. How close or far of a target are we in need of?"

"Accuracy and its maximum of distance combined and its detonation strength."

The fortress is situated on a summit overlooking a valley. It is only moving into the third period of the shadow and the fortress seems to be on the crest of it. This will not change. Akir is completely covered, and Kranaqus is one quarter. Zed is on the inner crest and will maintain a temperature of minus five and five Celsius. It fluctuates with solar flares and geothermal outlets, volcanic activity, geothermal spring runoffs. So dressing for this is not difficult.

They found themselves overlooking a void in the tree line a meadow that is at least twenty kilometres away along the forest there are some dead zones with stumps and rotting deadfall. These made easy targets and easy to see blasts. So they started firing into the closest to them on low settings.

“Oh, the difference of these in comparison to what we have is extreme. Let’s turn up the power and go for distance.” They walked over to the edge of the cliff and, looking over into the lower valley region, pointed to the fist deadfall.

“Turn it up to one-quarter power and fire into that pile of debris.”

When tech fired it, it turned the pile into a flaming blaze and smoke. They also saw that the diameter of the beam was larger.

“Oooooo… turn it up and, fire it into that deadfall on the other side of the river.” the lieutenant pointed out.

“OK.” Tech turned it to half-power knowing that the diameter would increase as well. “Wait. Let me make a suggestion. Instead of hitting these close-range objects why not go further, like, that mountain range behind the hill we’ve been firing on. The beam is set with a larger diameter so we’ll know where it’s hitting, and it will give a perspective of distance and accuracy.”

“Right, disarm it, so all we see is the area it hits and has no destructive force behind it. That way we can see the point of impact without giving away what we’re doing at this time. I want the captain to be here when we fire it, for effect.”

“OK,” he removed the core so that it only fired as a light beam. Setting up again he took aim and fired on the mountainside. The mountain was still inside the shadow crest and the beam would still be visible if it were big enough. But it was not. So the lieutenant told him, the tech, to increase it to the maximum. In doing so the beam would increase its diameter and be visible from their distance.

“Wow, this beam doesn’t skew from any point targeted. And the diameter remains constant.” The diameter of the beam was so large it lit up one-quarter of the mountainside. “Leave it now and we’ll go it to warm up and retrieve the captain.”

The captain was sitting at the fire in the kitchen drinking a hot beverage. Mulling over the map sitting in front of him, he looked up, “what have you discovered?”

“We’re set up on the cliff and overlooking the range behind the fortress. We have made some discoveries I think you’ll be impressed with.”

“Grab a cup and join me for a hot one.” the captain gestured. The lieutenant sat down by the fire to warm himself and join the captain.

Pointing to the map the captain began to go over what he has planned and explains why he needed to know the accuracy of distance when firing.

"I have been going over where they are camped and the hill's placement to our fortress. This is what I've assessed. We are here, they are here. In between, we have these hills that lead into the valleys and mountain ranges.

"We can use them as camouflage while making our way to these points. They are about five kilometres from their camp, yes it is colder in that region but that's what makes it so beautiful. They will not be expecting an attack from us during this period." He looked into the lieutenant's face to see if he was grasping the unique covert use of this period. To his knowledge it has never been done and, if successful, will set a whole new tactic in war strategies. They both looked at each other and the captain knew at that moment he understood.

"We have a chance to capture a foothold on Akir soil and set a new p precedence in strategies." they got up found the tech and went to test the power, even with the distance they were about to use. Setting it on one-quarter power they fired at the furthest target in the range of mountains.

"How far would you say that is?" the captain asked.

"About fifty kilometres." the tech interjected.

"Incredible and it didn't lose any power. Gather this and let's prepare one unit of twelve soldiers. They can break into three teams of four, when they reach the foothills, before the Akir camp, find the highest ground. It should take half a period to get there. What you want to do is find each power source and destroy them. The light emitting from the area tells me that there are at least six."

As they entered the fortress the captain continued, "You want to be at least twenty kilometres from camp, as you get further into the shadow you will be more susceptible to the cold, prepare for that. Optical instruments are your greatest assets take two for each team. The devices will do the job at half power; they are very accurate so making each shot count is important. Get out of there as fast as possible at that distance you have plenty of time to be back here before they reach the sight if they even try. They will have no heat or light and have no other choice but to retreat back to headquarters."

It took at least one period to ready the unit and get underway. There are only four periods left before the shadow ends if they can do this in two periods Akir and Kranaqus will have to fall back and arrange for another attack at some other time. Meanwhile, Zed can make a stronghold and occupy some territory inside Akir.

When there are confrontations between Kranaqus and Zed they are usually in the same regions unless they meet on the oceans. The mountains make changing the location of entering difficult and uncompromising. So the surprise is not usually expected because of this, Zed soldiers know the layout of the region and have a great idea of where they should set up.

They want to place themselves in three different locations so they can observe the camp's entirety. Each team will take out two generators and get back to the fort in separate units. That way being tracked will be much harder.

Except for the difficulty of ice and snow the plan went off flawlessly, each unit returned unscathed and the distant lights didn't return. Even after the shadow of Fauiq left the region there was no activity in the area.

Zed then began planning an occupation of the position but decided to wait until they knew what they might be confronted with, so they set up an observation post with minimal armament and personnel.

Chapter 17

Sit in Six

Axyan said, "I will not make the next sit-in so maybe it should be adjourned, and Umutt be taken to his destiny. There is an even number on the committee and that could easily end in a stalemate if we are not careful. So you have the time to take the moment to odd out the membership."

Fanyrottiss then remarked, "I have already taken that decision into account and expect only a single member turn out on that day. Harour is putting together the disposal chambers, and I'll be waiting for Umutt, which have been prepared for him and any others we need to consider."

Axyan sat back in his chair and contemplated the future of the committee, how is this going to play out? He questioned in thought, it isn't the idea of challenges outside the membership that is easily dealt with it's the committee itself, do I rely on the trust of the final three or do I act on my own? Taking on the information from the past and the changes in the committee, the Emperors elected and how they have been brought down, things are not always what they seem, and the fact that I'm not there right now makes a very important consideration to light, "what has Fanyrottiss got planned for me?" Axyan Began to wonder.

After packing he realised that there is extra time and he didn't have to leave immediately, so he went down to the manager and arranged to stay some extra few days so he could take advantage of the known taverns and seedy underworld in this district. Also, he would like to take some time to plan a different route back to avoid the Zyus that are so heavily populated in the area he first travelled.

He went out to check a tavern called Midnight, and since there is no midnight on any of the planets, it is an appropriate name for the time, all planets are in perpetual daylight as there are four suns. The only time there is an experience of darkness is when there's an eclipse by a lunar satellite or a planetary eclipse. We look forward to these times because it is the only time we can see the outer universe in great magnificence; otherwise, we are looking at the stars with telescopes.

So Axyan walks into the tavern and sits down to have a drink, he is there not more than an hour when he is approached by a female, "Hey, you're not the regular sod that comes around these parts, is ya?"

Looking at his drink he replied, "Well, I don't usually come this far to seek company or entertainment but I just happen to be in town for a few days on leave and thought I'd check out the social life of this community." as he looked up to see who he is talking to and smiled in his usual evil persuasive style.

"I'm intrigued by your manner, you create suspicion in your smile, what are you here for, business or fun, or are you planning to keep it a mystery?" she said stroking his arm as he sipped on his ale.

"Well, for now, I am interested in having something to eat and to continue watching the pole peelers, of which you happen to be sitting in the way of view, could you pull your chair around to the left please."

She did so with a reluctant jerkiness and then suggested, "I'll be on in a few, after the next two peelers, will you wait until after my performance, it's my last for the day. It's early and I'm wondering, if you're interested in having a little fun is on your mind."

He turned to speak just as his food is being served and said, "I've come for some food and a little fun, and from my observation, you seem to be well travelled in this region, are you not?"

She nodded yes.

And Axyan went on to say, "Well, I'm in need of finding a better way back to Rox, I don't care if it's longer but just that it's safer. If you could be of assistance and show me a different path, I would be very appreciative and show you my gratitude before I leave." at that point they made a mutual agreement and planned to meet at the back of the tavern after she ended her final set.

They walked back to his accommodation and ordered in some drink, and something to lighten the head, fodder, as its known, is to be smoked or eaten, but in its ingestion or inhalation it acts as an aphrodisiac and can create some very bizarre hallucinations.

Although they were naked they only frolicked together, without intimacy or foreplay. After the intensity of their fervour, they found themselves outside, still naked and still in a state of ominous dis culmination.

As Umutt sat waiting for the committee members to arrive he made some preparations for his participation for the election candidates, Fanyrottiss entered and started with "Umutt, it appears it's only us two today."

Walking across the room looking over the quart yard and continued, "There is something I need you to take care of can you come with me and we'll go over the particulars."

As they began walking, Umutt started, "Since the disappearance of Misric it has been very quiet and things haven't felt the same, have you noticed Fanay?"

His whole body was showing hesitance not because of the discussion but with the direction they were headed. The incineration disposal sites were not usual placed on the topic unless someone was in the process of inquisition or prepared for the disappearance.

"We are on the impasse of change, and there have to be some balances met with the imbalance of overture to the Emperor. This means that some of us have to be sacrificed in order to keep equity of discipline and structure."

Umutt knew where this was headed and wondered how he could escape the direction that Fanyrottiss was taking him, he needed an excuse to be dismissed for an hour that would give him enough time to execute his backup, he and Misric put together for just an occasion like this. The committee was never to be trusted he went into this membership with disdain and now it is being realised. With Misric gone he knew he was next, and now, what is the plan.

"There must be new faces presented to the people of Kranaqus So there have been arrangements made too," Umutt interjected.

"I don't mean to alarm you but there seems to be an awful lot of smoke maybe we should go back and investigate? Hmmmmm," said Umutt as he stood looking behind himself, after they got about half a mile from where they were an alarm went off, it was distinguishable as a fire alarm and, looking back, Umutt and Fanyrottiss saw that it was from their office building.

Panicking Fanyrottiss said, "We'll go over this later right now we need to get back and find out what is burning and how it's to be put out."

Even though there is some technology in this period of Qua there was still no real system set up to fight fires, outside there were ground hoses, but inside plumbing is made for design such as fountains, drinking veins, washrooms and kitchens, fires were rare, and for the most part, were controlled from the outside, so anything inside was usually not salvageable, and important documents were always lost unless stored in a separate part of the building or housed in an archives storage building separate from the office or department boards of the council.

Umutt grinds a little. He knew something was up in the council when Misric was announced dead, and before the sit-in, he planted a distraction to give him time to make his escape. While Fanyrottiss and Umutt were running back to the estate to check out what is burning Umutt took the opportunity and lost himself in the growing crowd. Fires always stirred a crowd, because it took a lot of people to put it out or just to maintain a controlling difference.

No one wants to have it spread throughout the building or beyond the perimeter of the sight that is burning. That could be disastrous for any part of the municipality, once out of control from the original start point, putting it out would be a tedious task, and major loss would follow in its wake.

After putting the fire out Fanyrottiss started looking around for Umutt, when he could not find him he began to grow suspicious about this whole event. Although there was a lot of smoke it turned out to be a minor circumstance, and when Fanyrottiss looked to find Umutt he could not be found, so he sent for, Babol, "Babol, you must find Umutt. He has information vital to the next election and must be found."

Being in charge of civil affairs his men would have free rein and finding him shouldn't be difficult if he is still in the city. He could not have gone far in this short time. Babol has been given strict orders that if there is any resistance to kill him. "Bring him to the disposal building for questioning and hold him until future notice."

Babol saluted and gathered some of his men to start searching the city.

Sit-in Seven

Axyon, upon returning to his accommodation with his companion, to work on his route back to Rox, discovers that things have been moved. He looks at her and her at him, the eyes tell everything, and there it is she has no idea who I am. She has just given away her deceit, I have been a committee member for twenty years, and I know when someone is lying.

"So, let's sit and go over the route I need to take," Axyon said while pulling out the map of Kranaqus.

These maps are only of specific areas, the Kranaqus maps are the most detailed because of the new technology, aerial views are much easier to decipher, and overall, above mapping is precise. The committee has made a point to have teams go out and map every inch of land on the globe. It has made campaigning a lot better for their armies and plotting trails over difficult terrain.

"I usually stick to the forests, although it isn't as safe, it has a familiarity about it that makes everything more reassuring," she exclaimed with assured confidence. "The desert can be crossed as you already know but you are easily seen by predators, as you also found out."

Axyon sat there staring at her, she is as cool as a tiger in its den, "*what is she setting me up for*?" He questioned in thought.

She went on, "You have that floating device, these trails will make it easier for travel but then you'll have to take a right to get back on the proper trail to Rox. Staying below the tree shield rather than above is the best way to travel; you are out of the sun, which can get excruciatingly hot at this time of the orbit, as you know we have three suns in the sky at any given time." She gestured, "it is a long way but safer." After a morning romp and brunch, she left, not in hurry, but in a questionable silence. Axyon then got on the communicator and called Fanyrottiss.

"Hey," he said sipping on a hot beverage, "I'm on my way back, and taking a different route, it's supposed to be safer but the person I was with offers some suspicion of question and I don't trust her. How did you make out with Umutt?" Axyon asked inquisitively.

"He disappeared, there was a fire at the estate, which turned out to be minor, it seemed set, like a diversion; anyway, he disappeared while I was checking it out. I summoned Babol to find him he should be found and dealt with before the next sit-in."

Babol sent for a squad of his men to pan out around the city and locate where Umutt might be hiding.

Umut quickly went home to gather some necessary notes and put together a travel bag for a fast and hasty exit. Trying to get out of the city before being missed the only mode to choose is the board, it's discreet and fast, Fanyrottiss will know he set the fire as a diversion when he sees how small it is, it only creates a large amount of smoke to appear as a big blaze, but when extinguished is realised as an intentional distraction.

Getting on his flat board he began to rise and seeing the smoke he knew they hadn't put out the fire. Wanting not to be detected he chose to remain low while moving through the streets until he got outside the city perimeters. Thinking to himself, “I made it!” when looking behind him he could still see the smoke and knew the search wouldn’t be carried out until they discovered it was a set-up.

Right now he had to think of where to go. He could no longer stay on the island or in Kranaqus. There is very little that goes on in Xyph, or the Islands, he has never ventured further than Ockuyu, and no one would suspect him to travel in that direction.

Babol, after a few hours, became frustrated his squadrons reported that Umutt was no longer in the city. “No, he must be on his way to somewhere unexpected, a place that is not familiar to us or any others. Is there somewhere he, Babol, could think of? An area that is not regularly used, a place not for vacationing, or where family is known to be residing.”

It took him a while but then.

“Yes, there is… the province Xyph. It is northern enough that temperatures are extreme and are not a usual vacationing location. The population is low and the forest is vast one could easily get lost and stay off the grid. The land is plentiful, one could remain hidden with no question of who they are, or if they might be running from anything.”

Looking at his men he suggested that he send two different squads one to the east into Akir to cover any chance that he might have gone to his family for refuge or hold up until he could figure a different plan. And one to the west just in case he had the idea that he would not be sought out in that region.

“Right.” Babol, cried out, “We shall search until no rock has been unturned. He will be found and brought alive to you before the next election.”

“No,” said Fanyrottiss.

“Dead or alive, preferably dead. He has not got the censorship to remain out of the public eye. His personality will come forward just to remain a part of the status quo. So, unless he gives up willingly then deceased is preferred.” Looking at Babol strait in the eyes, “Yes sir” He retorted turned and was off. The two squads met back at the estate front entrance where Babol gave them orders to locate Umutt at all cost and not to return without a body dead or alive.

“If he resists preferably dead. I want one squad to the east and on to the west if you need more to cover the east grab another squad. If the west is difficult, as it is highly unexplored, you can also grab another ten privates in the search you will report back every week until he is found, dismissed.”

Axyon started to prepare to leave, and as he was getting on the flat board he began thinking of the strange behaviour of the peeler. She was almost ghost-like with the distance she put between the two of them. Dismissing it he just got on his board and left.

Sit-in Eight

Axyon arrived early, When Fanyrottiss walked in he was preparing an agenda for the next sit-in, Fanyrottiss then asked, "Why were you not at the last sit-in?" with a scornful look on his face.

Looking up at him Axyon said, "That is an interesting question, and the story I'm going to tell you will answer it quite gamely."

Taking his eyes off him and continuing with his writing. "While I was in Ockuyu I had a few days grace and decided to check out the social life, so I went down to a peeler tavern to eat and be entertained. Before getting my food a female sat down beside me and asked if she could join me until her next set. I said OK.

"During our conversation, we got to know each other fairly well and in discovering that she is well-travelled in this region I asked her if she could help me plan a safer route back to Rox. She agreed and told me to wait at the back of the bar until she finishes her last set. So I did. We spent the rest of the day drinking and carousing at different bars and taverns.

"She knew which had sweet deals for beverages and other things. You know what I mean; anyway, we were so heavily intoxicated we found ourselves outside running around naked, like a tree in the cold season. When we finally came to our senses we were back at my lodging. We discovered a few days had past and I had to leave to make sit-in seven, as did she, to her next gig.

"So she helped me to work out a trail that avoided the desert, but it would be longer by doing that, yet I would still make the meeting. I believe the time we shared made me vulnerable to her suggestions because I didn't think that this female was not to be trusted and you would think I would have more awareness to someone's deceit. Well, I didn't, and I'm not proud of the next phase of the story," he said looking straight into Fanyrottiss eyes.

"The next morning, I left early, and for the first stretch of the journey, it went very smooth, even though I saw a couple of Zyus flying overhead, they were quickly out of the picture as I left their territory. Everything was going great into the afternoon, but then I started noticing bones. Just a few strewn around the ground nothing to be concerned with and all animals so it looked like a hunter's playground. But it started to get heavier and some were natives, and as I got future into the forest the natives' bones became thicker, it looked somewhat like a combat graveyard.

"I continued and cresting the hill I noticed a swarm about two miles away. They didn't look threatening so I ventured further into the area, and when I was about half a mile away I saw clearer what was happening. A group of dracos had been passing through, just as a swarm of red ires were hatching. The Dracos, a mother and her cubs five beasts in all, were covered with them.

"That's when I realised why the area was so laden with bones. Although the animal bones outnumbered the natives, there were still a questionable number of them. I realised then the peeler was setting me up. I don't carry large sums of money, so, it had to be for my platform.

"That's all it could be. Anyway, I went back on my original route, taking up more travel time and, having to hide from the Zyus flying overhead, made the way back more hazardous than originally planned."

"What about the peeler," asked Fanyrottiss.

"I spent about a day looking for her, but was unsuccessful, so I just came back. She's a peeler I'll be able to find her once we're finished with the election." Axyon said, walking around the room in frustrated curiosity.

"What of Umutt?" he asked, looking out over the grounds outside the building.

"He's still yet to be recaptured but we have four squads out on his trail, two to the east as far as Zed, and two to the west into Xyph." Butting out his stogie and blowing the smoke to the ceiling from the couch.

"Well, let's hope that has a quick resolve. We don't need any loose ends now, do we. We have a couple of days before the next sit-in lest hope for good reports on all fronts."

The three remaining members showed up a little late so the sit-in got started half hour later than usual.

"We have a guest today although he hasn't shown up yet he will be here momentarily," said Fanyrottiss seating himself at the table.

"Meanwhile, we'll just go over the last meetings minutes," as Harour was halfway through the minutes Babol stepped into the room, Fanyrottiss motioned for him to sit and he did, after the minutes Fanyrottiss got up, "Our guest has arrived and now I will turn the meeting over to Babol, please give your update on the whereabouts of Umutt."

“Well, I wish I could give good news but he has vanished, it’s like he was prepared for this and had a destination ready to run to. The search will continue until he is found but that could take more time than thought at first. There are two squads, split into four teams, in the field right now and we are preparing to send more. If in two weeks, he is not found there will be more sent out. But, I believe that what we have is sufficient and he will be found.”

Babol stood looking at the three faces, waiting for a response from the committee, and was finally asked, “What kind of preparations have been made for the election’s security?”

Harour asked, “And do you know what the disposal and refuse building sight is like?”

He continued, “I have security officers at both locations the facilities are running within standards set by the municipality it is a difficult area to keep up but the new technology is a great source of help making the hauling and dumping of garbage a much easier task than in the past. “Babol went on to include “as for the election, there have been special securities made in regards to each facility ballots are set to be received in, also the dates for debates outside have towers that are being set up in those areas and the indoor areas like the arena and auditoriums are mapped out with the placement of officers and communications experts, if you would like the reports and maps of all structures they can be made available in a few weeks but I have to go over them first to make sure everything is in order then I can have copies sent to you. Does that sound agreeable? Otherwise, you can receive the preliminary pages in two days after I copy them.”

“I think if you can arrange to have them sent to us in the next few days your first draft will be acceptable,” said Axyon, “that way we can make preparations for our beginnings of debates and speeches.”

“If that will be all I would like to be dismissed and get back to my duties,” said Babol looking around the room.

“Yes, but keep us informed. Umut’s whereabouts are very important, if he is discovered I want him brought back alive, death would be a presumption of accidental collateral damage. We will have a new business for you involving the competition. Who they are and, where they can be found.

“I would like you to put together a team to look for these collaborators so we can know who we are dealing with before the time of presentations,” said Fanyrottiss.

“OK,” replied Babol, as he left the room.

"Now back to the business at hand, when having we scheduled to meet with our candidates?" asked Fanyrottiss turning pages to find the date or an empty space to slot it onto a section for future consideration.

"Six weeks from now," answered Harour.

"Good, that gives time to have Babol find Umutt and the opposition," implied Fanyrottiss.

* * *

Sora met Tumi at the tavern and as they sat for a beverage Sora began to explain, "There is a place in the janitor's department. It's hidden behind a wall with a cabinet in front of it. We don't have to be there to know what is being said at the meetings. All we have to do is pick up the disc, from the vowel, and then we have the meeting complete insight. Tumi smiled and asked, "Do you have the disc now?"

"No, I have to get it tonight. When I was there earlier the security was doing rounds and compromised the storage room. They spent, at least two hours there. It was as though they were directing taking stock. Because I'm new they, don't have me do that. But it seems, there is always secure with the administrator when taking count."

Sora, after ejecting the disc, set up a meeting with Tumi at her place, "There has been a new development into the committee. It seems that two of the members are missing or dead. The captain Babol has four teams out searching for them and one team looking for us."

"This is a good thing," Tumi exclaimed. "They will be in the neighbouring towns and rural areas leaving us to roam the streets without scrutiny."

They both sat to listen to the meeting in its entirety.

"Hmmmm," Tumi began to contemplate this information, "perhaps we should be thinking of changing our base. We might be too close to Rox to keep from being discovered. There is a beach, outside of Rox, that has several caves where we could set up and we would go undetected for the duration. I'll bring this to Je-hu's attention when I see he's next."

Sora nodded in agreement and getting up to fix a beverage, gesturing to Tumi to join her he nodded, no, she added, "I know the place you speak of, I used to go there years ago just for some alone time and to contemplate where my life's journey is going to take me. When we do that it will give us escape options as well."

As she went to the cooler, Tumi sat and contemplated this observation and began liking the idea more.

Chapter 18
The Celebration

If You

If you
Believe in heaven
You must
Believe in hell
To
Believe in the
Devil
Or GOD
Is your spell

If you wish
Upon a falling star
If you ponder
About where you are
If your choice
is unopened doors
The mask you wear
Is to venture the dare

Can you believe
In aiming higher
Then where
You are
Keeping in mind
The sense of time
And where you
Find yourself

They all met back at the meeting place and started going over the names that were retrieved. Naveen started to explain why she grabbed two extra names.

"While I was fingering my way through the files I began to notice that there were more potential candidates than first thought. So I did more searching, into several other towns and discovered more and realised that there is something wrong with these numbers. Seeing this, I thought that we have to do more digging into the conspiracy theory that Je-hu has suggested, because, it looks like he's right," Naveen insisted.

As she sat on the floor she began laying out the folders and exposing the names she recovered, which contained medical histories and education.

Just as Je-hu walked into the place, he hadn't heard anything from the team and looked at them puzzled, "Where's Ohn-ohn?" he asked sternly, looking at the both of them. "And who is this?"

Grabbing Misric by the throat and almost breaking his neck.

"Hold off their smart man, this is Misric, say hello to one of the committee members." Je-hu almost gutted Nayrr right there, until Naveen grabbed his wrist.

He sternly said, "Listen to the story, you red ire, if it wasn't for us he would be dead right now, so settle down and shut up."

Je-hu loosened his grip on Misric and sat down. "When we were finished gathering what we needed at the historical archives we were on our way back to Ohn-ohn whom we had to leave on the first level of the emergency corridor exit because he got injured on the way in, at the entrance," said Nayrr, with purpose.

"He fell down the ladder because it was old and dried out, so by the time we got to the next entrance he was in too much pain to continue. So we left him."

"At his insistence," Naveen interjected.

"Anyway, when we got back to him red ires had cocooned him and ingested him." Nayrr, shrugged.

"There was nothing we could do." Naveen interjected again. "We had to leave him."

Nayrr then continues, "As we were leaving the corridor we saw that some of the committee members were entering the building, but as they did so they lingered a while outside and we could hear them talking about one of their members being set up to be ambushed. They were very candid about it, not thinking that they might be overheard, any way they mentioned where it was going to happen, before entering and that's when Naveen said she knew where the location is and we devised a plan to rescue this member because we felt that he might come in handy during the campaign, with inside information. This member would know everything we need to challenge the committee's candidate and help us win."

"Why is he so stiff?" asked Je-hu with a puzzled look.

"We don't know he was like this when we grabbed him, so let's give him some time and maybe he will become more coherent," said Naveen pinching his face and staring into his eyes.

"So, Ohn-ohn couldn't be saved. Hey."

"He was crawling with them; you know what they do to their prey."

Nayrr continued, "His death was not in vain, we have some great material to go over and I think we'll find exactly what we need."

They all sat together in contemplation while they looked over the files.

"Here," said Naveen, "Zavita has an excellent profile. She's been elected to serve in the mountainous region of Kaya. She has a very good history of budgeting for that region and has been very outspoken with the taxation of the people which has cost her some financial setbacks. Zavita has also been pleading to the council for army support in that area, because of the villainous environment there needs to be a stronger presence of policing.

"Even though the population is low it is a very hostile region and, before Zavita was elected, there were many assassinations of previous ministers. She is well known and, I think, an easy turn for this assignment."

"OK, that's one," said Je-hu discard the other female and focus on the male candidates, "we need two, and you have five to choose from," He went on "one has to be independent of the rest of the candidates so we need a strong character in that position. We need to discover what happens when there is true opposition in place of the committee's potentials."

Looking at Je-hu, Naveen objected with, "no, I think I should interview both to, have some backup, we don't know how any of these candidate's potential or how they are going to respond, and I can be quite persuasive when I want something to happen or someone to be involved."

"OK," Je-hu replied. "Have it your way, just make sure we have at least one to work with, right."

"Right," she replied.

They all sat around and took the folders before them and started reading. Tumi, started to exclaim about another, "Jyati," holding up the folder, "he is from the Pazar twins region and has been in place for twelve rotations. He has been very outspoken about the abuse of comity involvement of regions and taxation."

"Intez also looks like a fine candidate, so let's go over all the files first and then vote on whom we think should be running, and we haven't even approached them about this. We don't even know if they might be interested," said Je-hu

“I think what we should do is get them in a place and bring them into the plan giving them the decision to accept or oppose a placement in this plan,” Naveen interjected.

“Wouldn’t this meeting expose us as traitors and give the opportunity to being discovered,” implied Naveen.

“Well, you chose some very excellent candidates, they are all very outspoken and disgruntled at the way things are seemingly dictated by the comity.” Je-hu implied looking at the folders in front of him.

“Why don’t we go meet them on a one to one and find out just how angry they are, Naveen, you can talk to the women, Tumi and I will talk to the males. Let’s do this as quickly as possible do you think we need one or two weeks,” he asked looking around.

“Given the distances, I think two weeks would be the right choice of time,” said Tumi, with Naveen nodding in agreement.

“OK, two weeks.” agreed Je-hu. “Even though I have agreed to do these interviews I must remind you that I cannot be exposed and must stay on the side-lines as much as possible. So, Tumi you will take three of the five male candidates and I will take two, agreed.” Tumi shook his head yes and they both separated the pile, two to Je-hu and three to Tumi.

Elected members are chosen for the intervention of the Emperor’s throne, for Je-hu’s team of conspirators.

F - Zavita
F - Azoz
M - Intez
M - Jyati
M - Samar
M - Esyr
M - Iymad

Chapter 19

Naveen, after putting together an escort of two guards and three beasts carrying provisions, was ready to set out the next day. Her first interview would be with Azoz, she is more interested in Zavita, so she wants to save her as the second interviewee, because, she anticipates a more productive and intense association to the plan.

Azoz lives on the mountain of Kaya and is the father of the two so Naveen set out to kaya first in the town of Quirec south. Because the travel is quite harsh, by that I mean to say, the forests are filled with dangers. Trees called Encarta are very thick in some places they stand very tall and there is usually five daises (platform petals) to each tree. In the middle of every dais, there is a cup, it can be any colour and held in the flower cup it holds the most incredible nectar.

When used as a resource for ingestion: to drink, it has healing properties and nectar has a very divine and intoxicating essence that people would die for. And they do because once you step onto the dais you are doomed. The tree allows you to take a drink from its flower, there is always enough, and then the dais envelops the intruder, there is no escape.

The nectar is so enticing people go mad and die trying to drink it. There have been some very good inventions to capture the nectar and sell it and, due to its overwhelming toxicity, is very successful with its exploit.

Another danger is a crawling plant with poisonous thorns, called the thorn crawler. This plant depends on the immune system of the victim, for most of the poisonous creatures, flying and land crawlers; there is a vaccine if you haven't got enough antibodies to fight the infection. With the vaccine, it becomes a little infection, easily taken care of.

The flying creatures are unpredictable so it's best she protects herself with an immune enhancer. It's not hundred per cent but, as it's been stated. The creatures are unpredictable, that's why extra protection is necessary, but its cost is high. Still, it's number one on the need to have for travel list.

Naveen chose to travel by beast, until she gets to the edge of the forest, at the mid-way stretch of the mountain. She will then use, the new technology of, the platforms the rest of the way. After she sets camp of course. Sleeping outside (in tents) has a specific way, you don't sleep on the ground, because crawling insects are very aggressive and get into everything no matter how tight.

So everything hangs, it's a very easy setup. First, there are four corners posts to plant; depending on the angle of the posts determines the tautness of the hammock. There are different heights as well. The hammock has to be at least five inches above the ground, the reason being invaders. These are insects that feel warm-blooded animals and invade their bodies.

They begin by starting to eat the liver then lay eggs which continue the process of slowly eating the victim from the inside out. They begin as larva, becoming adults then laying more eggs and the cycle begins all over again until the body is devoured. This takes as long as two weeks in some cases, and you don't even know until it's too late. The only way to prevent this is with hanging beds.

Since using the new platform technology at the historical building and feeling, not just seeing, how these things work. She is comfortable with them and is finally ready to try one. But only on open areas with little or no obstacles, so above the tree line is the safest way to handle a first-time outdoor effort.

Each mountain has a different tree line, Kaya's ends at 7,500 feet. The platforms seemed easy enough, but manoeuvring around objects is straining. The riding beasts will remain behind with her escorts, she will go in alone.

Now that she's ready to leave. The first course of the journey will take one week; Kaya is a tall mountain and the forest. Naveen has to travel, which is dangerous. Her first day was uncompromising, and setting up camp was fast and easy. It's the next three-day stretch that holds the complications; there will be little time for rest due to the season. It's moving into the storming season just before planting and reproduction.

Things have a way of disappearing during this time and are never seen or heard from again, so caution and swiftness is the order of travel here. As she started to walk around the camp her rear escort seemed a little slow with the gathering routine, so she thought to roust him to get things in focus for the day's journey. He was the second on watch and might have taken time to catch a few winks of sleep; this would not be a good time because of the flying parasites during this period of rotation. But that is not the circumstance, he is rapt.

This is the first stage of hyper animation caused by a parasite that flies around looking for a host. The fastest way to make this happen is to sting the back of the neck, of the victim, and deliver the venom directly into the bloodstream using the main artery to the brain. This ensures a quick immobilisation and Riga-mortise like state of being. This is only temporary and lasts a few hours, the victim then recovers and can carry on while, unknowingly, the eggs that were implanted at the stem of the brain begin to feed off the nerves and brain.

The way it's detected is by a bruise that's left under the left or right ear. It only stays for a few days then disappears and is not seen again. Then symptoms start to show, starting with unbalanced movements, slurred communications and poor eyesight. There is no remedy for this and trying to remove the parasites from the brain stem results in full-body paralysis and death.

The team began towards the forest's end where they planned to set up camp again, while moving through the trees Naveen started to notice strange behaviours from one of her escorts.

"What's going on with Xyx?" she asked the rear guide. "He's acting a little drunk."

"I don't know, why we don't have an examination of all of us to check for parasites, it seems the most likely thing," said Cyd.

So, stripping naked, Naveen and Cyd checked each other and found nothing, after dressing, they called for Xyx. They didn't have to look far upon their first exam they discovered the bruise left by a Xyxus.

"He's doomed," said Cyd, turning to look at Naveen. "There's nothing we can do but carry on and, when the time comes, make his finally a painless one. But we cannot let these parasites escape, there is a lake before the forests end, a mile before our second camp. Dead or alive I suggest we put it out there, the water is the only way to stop these things from spreading out into the atmosphere."

"OK," replied Naveen. "I know of this lake."

As the team was walking through the forest Cyd started to hear Xyx hum, turning to look at Naveen he implied, "It's starting to happen," Naveen looked behind her and saw Xyx skipping, and somewhat dancing like a little kid, she found it cute, and the whistling and humming made an arduous journey a little lighter. As they neared the small lake there was a sudden thump behind them, both Cyd and Naveen turned at the same time to discover Xyx had collapsed.

"They knew they only had a few hours to get him into the water of the small lake, or there would be a swarm of Xyxus flying in the area, and that is not good. The first few days of their short life is not lethal, but after they reach maturity they start to look for hosts. Once he is placed in water, and it has to be deep at least three metres. Even though the larva can still hatch the pressure would not allow them to spread their wings and float to the top where they could start to swarm.

"How deep is the lake in the middle?" asked Cyd.

"Deep enough to drown a Dracos," said Naveen.

After taking Xyx to the middle of the lake and sending him to the bottom, with a few well-placed rocks, they went back to gather their stuff and carry on. As they continued to the end of the forest, they did so in silence. While beginning to set up camp, on the edge of the forest, Naveen said she wanted to wait till the next day before leaving so she could gather the materials she wanted to take with her. It will take at least two days to get there, then she would have to search throughout the town to find where Azoz lives.

The next day she left early, on her flat board, the open freedom above the treeline felt so excitingly riveting that she began to take chances by flying low around singled out trees. As sparse as they might have been there were a few above the tree line that she could play with. Her flat board moved so fast she realised she would be at Quirec sooner than planned.

Entering the township her first order is to find accommodation and the first place she knew of, as she had been there on many an occasion, is her favourite haunt. The Dracos Inn, she knew everyone there and she was sure, though it had been at least ten rotations since the propriety would still be the same. Things change little in these outer regions. Walking in it felt different and the native at the counter was also different.

"Hey," Naveen said hesitantly, looking around she got an uneasy feeling; everyone in the room stared as though she had just interrupted a private conversation and she felt an icy chill run through her veins.

Walking over to the bar she felt that a few drinks would relax her enough to get a better feel for the place and give her the right mind to get a room and hold up here for the few days she intended to stay. "An orange star," she said to the bartender, throwing it back, she ordered two more and then asked, "Has this place gone through a change of ownership?"

He looked at her and making a stern face asked, "Have you been in before?"

Taking a sip of the O-star as it was generally called, "Yes when I was a medic and travelled to this region as a specialist. But, that was ten years ago and I haven't been in this area for that time since."

"What brings you here now?" he asked, "pleasure, or business?"

She replied, "Pleasure."

Not wanting to give away her reasons for being there, "Then I guess you don't know what happened five rotations back" glancing up at her.

"No, I didn't hear anything happening in this location, I've been busy."

"Well," he began, "There was an ownership dispute, the past owner had borrowed some money, but didn't look into who they were borrowing from. As it turned out the lenders were not legal and things went bad financially for the owners and paying off the borrowed money became an issue.

"When they went to readjust their account they were met with an adverse reaction and foreclosure. Dissatisfied with the decision, and realising their mistake, and finding the company was not legitimate they resolved to battle in a more traditional way and found some allies with some people who were also backstabbed by this lending agency, and proceeded to engage in a war of ownership and revenge. Anyway, they lost, and as you can see, the agency is the new owners and everything has changed. I'm now managing the bar, and my sister is managing the guests."

"What happened to the owners?" she questioned.

"Deceased," he said looking right into her eyes.

"Oh," she replied starting on her third o-star. She then got up from her seat, left the establishment and sought another place to be. She really liked the old owners and was disappointed to hear that they had been replaced in the manner it had happened. After cruising around, purchasing a map, and something to snack on, she found a place outside the urban area and settled in.

After spending the afternoon going over the map, she discovered where Azozs residence and office is. Not wanting to take the chance of limiting her time with an office visit she decided to make a house call that way she would be able to have a longer presentation time and get an appropriate response time. Finding her way through the streets she located the residence of Azoz and knew she had to wait until she returned.

Upon her return she a few hours later she was invited in and spent several hours going over her proposal and getting the inevitable "no" for the answer she felt completely drained and it was a waste of time. Going back to her accommodation she decided to leave immediately so her accompaniment and started off for Makir.

She knew she would have to enter the forest again and that meant parasites and bugs and other creatures. She looked at Cyd and said, “I think we should stay above the treeline as long as possible to avoid the creatures in the forest.”

He answered, “We’ve already lost one so I agree, we can follow the tree line almost halfway there but it will be hard riding because the trails are sketchy or non-existent.”

“Yes, that’s true, so I thought of an idea. We can travel above tree line for as far as we can then set camp and I can flat board to Makir and return to you after the presentation. Yes?”

“OK, but that will make the journey a lot longer,” answered Cyd looking at the ground.

“Yet, it will actually make the provisions last longer and your time getting there and back shorter” looking up and smiling. Then we best get on our way.” Naveen insisted and started along the open ground a barely noticeable path that followed the tree line.

It took two and a half days to get to a flat area. Where they set up camp, made dinner and got ready to sleep. In the morning, after a hot beverage, she left. Her flat board kept her above the trees and she could see exactly where she needed to go, what a great way to travel. Very little is needed, and the only thing to consider is bad weather, and at this time of the season, it’s rare. Just on that thought alone, Naveen started thinking, “*How do you combat the weather on one of these things.*”

She knew she wouldn’t be into Makir until the morning. After flying throughout the late PMs and early AMs, that’s going to make it a day and a half, cutting out on a lot of time. As she entered the city she found a place to lodge and rested. When she awoke it was early afternoon and she had to find a map and start looking for Zavita’s residence, her plan was the same as Azoz.

’s residence. It makes the interview more personable and less rushed. It took her most of the afternoon to find the map she needed and went back to her room to study it. Naveen knew that going there today was out of the question so she resolved to wait until after business hours the next day. After finding where she needed to be the next day, she stepped out again and went to a nearby tavern for something to eat, then returned for a good rest until the next day.

She spent the morning in the same tavern, as the night before, for her morning meal. Then getting on her board she got out the map and began the affirmation of Zavita finding her way through the streets was no easy task, if she went too high she couldn't read the signs and staying at street level had many obstacles, and trying to avoid them always lead to another obstruction. When she arrived at her destination she was surprised to find someone there, so she went to the door and knocked, "Hello," the person behind the partially open door asked.

"Good morning," answered Naveen. "I'm looking for Zavita, have I got the right residence?" asked Naveen as she peered inside the dwelling for confirmation of personage.

"Yes, but she is not here at the moment, she'll be back after 4:30 pm. If you come back at that time, she'll be here."

Naveen didn't want to press for more information, so she accepted the reply and left. She continued to do a tour around the city so she could get a better feel about where she is, then returned to the tavern for a few drinks, and a bite. Returning to her accommodation she decided to rest before meeting with Zavita.

Naveen arrived at Zavita's house at 6 pm, knocking on her door she wondered about Je-hu and how he might be getting on with his second interview, knowing he is taking all the risk by exposing himself to the potential candidates. Just then the door opened and Zavita said, "Hello, I've been expecting you my sister, who was here this morning, told me about your inquiry what is it you're in need of?" she asked gesturing to her inside.

Naveen then introduced herself and finding a seat in the living room started with her interview. After a few hours of questions and answers, she told her not to make a decision today and to take some time between now and tomorrow before she left to give an answer. Naveen also included that she is the first person she had in mind as the one to run for Emperor and hoped that she would agree to meet with the other candidates in the next few weeks. She would be back the next night for her answer and left on her board to where she is staying.

The next afternoon, after spending the day muddling about, she met with Zavita and got a negative response, but before leaving she gave her card and told Zavita, she had three weeks and if she changed her mind she could communicate on the frequency in under her name, or just show up at by using the map on the reverse side. Disappointed she got on her board and started on her way back to Rox.

More correspondence, this one to a citizen whom he has a son with; he was not planned but is an intentional birth to keep Je-hu in her life.

Hello, my enchantress,

Because there has been so many questions and reasons between us about what and why we have made the choices we are in now, all I have is patients and admiration for you. If it means losing you to someone else then I can only accept that decision from you and be as much a part of Nyman's life as I can. He is an important part of both of us and we can work together to make him understand that. It seems the longer I am away the farther away you both become. And, though we can talk, when I'm on Devi, the distance is always going to be a major factor and as you have already said your world is different now. So maybe we are growing apart or maybe you are growing into a different world or maybe…?

I don't know what it is you want to have except that education is important to you. Patience is all I have, three months is the time, I'm amazed that you and Nyman could feel so separated in such a short time and your mother is right, I should just let it all go, I don't know.

So I will just do what I have to do and wait, but at the same time, not stagnate. It is very disturbing that all these people think they can use this time to make you feel that I'm the wrong person for you and give no support. Though you have said you want us to work it out, it is in secret and so there, for me, is doubt. They make like who you're with is the great companion and he is so immature about who you are and how you like to spend your time. Whatever the outcome only time can tell, but for now, it's letters.

All I know is I miss you both, your laugh, his energy and the time we shared even the bad I miss because you were there and it turns out to be true. Even bad attention is better than nothing at all.

Love always, Je-hui. Hugs and kisses to both. Xxxoxo.

Chapter 20

Sit-in Nine

As they all arrived, at the same time, they fidgeted with the agenda and waited for Fanyrottiss to start, "Well, we know the other two won't be here we may as well get things moving, Harour can you go over the minutes of the last meeting." as he did so Fanyrottiss pulled out some papers and set them on the table. Harour finished the minutes and looked up, "We can continue with the old business or just move on to the new, it's your call," he said looking at Fanyrottiss.

Fanyrottiss replied, "Yes, we may as well move on to the new, I have before me three applications for candidacy for Emperor. Now as you know there doesn't have to be anything other than a written form with no names, no addresses, just a notary stamp. Everything else will be known at the beginning of the first week of the introductions and date setting for debates and interviews. So, let us go over who we have for our entries."

Sitting down he passed the speaking time over to Axyon. "We have our three candidates, Mahed of Rox, Sadia of Kaya, and Hazatt of Ysolda. They will be arriving in six weeks on Sit-in twelve that gives us another six weeks, before the beginning of the interviews and debates, to prepare our campaign with each of the candidates. Each one will have a different doctrine, in this way we can discover where the people stand in their thinking and we can pursue a more distinctive way of representation. Agreed?"

All answered, "Agreed."

"Now, I would like to go into some old unresolved business, Umutt, he hasn't been discovered as yet and I would like Bobal in for either the next sit-in or the following one for updates all in favour." They all raised their hand. "Great I'll set upon having him here. Is that all or is there another business to be considered?"

Nothing was suggested, and so the meeting was brought to an end, until the next sit-in, in two weeks.

Sit-in Ten

Entering the conference room, they all sat down and just stared at each other. Finally, Axyon said, "We know today's the day, right, "a silent pause, "which of the candidates is going to be with whom, that is the question. Do we draw straws, put names in a hat, or does any of you know who you want to work with and under what party constitution you want to follow?"

Fanyrottiss interjected with, "I've been thinking, I would like to work with Sadia and because she is from Kaya, which has a more social municipal direction we will take the Democratic forum, it will be a new ideology, business and social awareness, that would put a greater perspective into her thinking and a stronger presentation to the citizens of Kranaqus."

"OK," Axyon gestured, "All in favour," all raised their hands, "so passed."

The reason it was an easy acceptance is females do not have a strong position in this society. That's why, when in a political position they genuinely choose the social-political policy, with the idea of social reform or intervention, to increase education, awareness and hopeful citizen equality and political involvement by females.

Harour then inquired "I have been mulling over the candidates and would like to work with Mahed, he is from Rox and I would be more familiar with his insight to the political forum and would probably be the one elected because of our alliance."

"And under what political forum would you like to run?" questioned Axyon.

"Under Liberal, leadership with the understanding of continuing financial freedom and corporate stability, small business reform and industrial non-culpability."

"So be it," said Axyon, "all in favour?"

All raised their hand.

So, ordered, "And that leaves Hazatt to me" Axyon looked at the two of them and said, "I don't know if he is going to be happy with the social forum but someone has to bring it to the citizens as an opposition to change, but could we not bring to their attention something different, Conservative, which brings attention to the idea of less taxation to the citizen, more to the corporation, culpability to industry and the empire, can this be acceptable? All in favour?"

All hands raised.

"OK then, so passed. Conservative is the third forum. Meeting adjourned; we'll all meet bake here in two weeks."

They all left in disquiet conjecture.

Sit-in Eleven

They all walked into the conference room together sat at the table and again just stared at each other for at least five minutes before Harour said, "I propose we adjourn this meeting as, I am not prepared to submit my candidate's forum to date and I believe you are all in the same position. So, all in favour to adjourn until next meeting," they all raised their hand and they promptly got up and left.

Sit-in Twelve

Harour, was sitting, waiting for the rest of the committee to show as they did he objected, "I think we should make a new time or adjourn to the next meeting, I still need more time to put together my platform for my party candidate."

"As do I," said Axyon looking at Fanyrottiss.

"Well, it seems as though we are all on the same page, but as you both know, they arrive in two weeks and it is in our best interest that we have everything prepared."

He looked around and continued saying, "Before you all leave, I would like to note that in my hand I am holding the applications of your competition. These are only the pages of the application, and as you know they don't have to have any names only their intent to run for the Emperor's seat. The only time they need to expose themselves is at the beginning of the first week of debates.

"Get your ideology in order and put your opening arguments into perspective, this is not going to be an easy win. Even with the disappearances of one or two of the opposition they cannot all meet the same fate, so keep in mind that one or two will be running to the end of voting and can overpower the decision, all in favour of dismissing today's meeting."

They all raised their hands.

"None opposed."

They all left to continue their portfolio and meet back in two weeks.

* * *

Sora and Tumi sat listening to the recordings, they looked at each other, with a sense of relief, knowing that they haven't been discovered yet.

“Well, they have their candidates.” Tumi made understood “We have their names and we can access their records in the local historical building. But, I think that unnecessary.”

“Why, if we have a better understanding of who they were before their candidacy we will improve our knowledge of how to approach our arguments and speeches.” Sora expressed with insightfulness.

“Yes, but we already know the ideology of the parties, so if we stay on the subject the only thing working for or against us is, the charisma of the candidate.”

Tumi exclaimed, looking into his beverage, “Well, as it seems to be at this time, they are not even ready for opening. So, all we can do is work on our submissions and hope that we have stronger personalities. Let’s go find Je-hu and inform him of what we have uncovered, which isn’t much, but it’s a start and gives him a chance to comment.”

Tumi got up, after finishing his drink and walked to the door. “Good work, you did replace the disc didn’t you?” he questioned.

“Yes, of course, if anything they’ll let us know what their next moves are and we’ll be able to counter it with a full out war,” Sora said smiling.

“Watch your back, and we’ll set this up again,” she closed the door, and Tumi started on his way back to his residence.

Sit-in Thirteen

The candidates were the first to arrive, as they started to sit around the table Fanyrottiss started to pull out some paperwork and place it on the table, looking around the table and smiling he began, “What I have in front of me are the names of the opposition, this gives us an insight to discovery. What I mean by that is, we can find the background of each candidate and play them, also who of them is the most dangerous.

“So I have brought in, an outside resource who will seek out the past of each conflicting individual, by the next meeting we should have enough on each to criticise their motives and intent. I would like to introduce to you the one who will bring the opposition to us, please enter,” in through the door behind Fanyrottiss came a small unassuming dwarf-like being looking sheepish in character, with a heavy stature.

“I would like you to meet Kalex. He has worked in archives for the past forty-five rotations and has the knowledge of all that is on the registrar of the population. Because these candidates are known, finding their histories will be frustrating but simple, it may take time, but in the end, it will be worth it. So," handing out the pages of each of the candidates the committee has selected "you can go to Kalex. You have two weeks to obtain the information we need and, I expect you back here with each one's portfolio." Kalex left through the same door he entered and the committee continued their meeting.

"I realise that we haven't had Bobal in for his update on Umut so I took the initiative to get the information from him and bring it to all of you. Bobal believes Umut is in Xyph. He has been in hiding. Bobal's troops have been as far east and south as they could possibly get and there has been no sign of him. Xyph hasn't been overlooked, but because it was too obvious, it was saved till last. It is the most likely place he went. We think one of the islands. So he is going to be a hard find. But the good thing is, he won't compromise the election with rhetoric or argument."

The Committees accepted candidates for the election to the Emperor's seat:

m	Mahed, of Rox
f	Sadia, of Kaya
m	Hazatt, of Ysolda

* * *

Tumi, Sora and Aa-z sat at Sora's residence and began playing the recordings. It was like sharing secrets or eavesdropping on a potential victim. They got comfortable and started with where they left off.

"Well, it seems that Umut has fled, and they are spending a lot of time looking for him. There is fear in their words. I think they wonder what he is up to, if we could find him we would have another ally with our candidates," Sora exclaimed.

"Yes, but there is no time. We need to put together our subject matter contentions for each of the candidates, and prepare for the rallies," Tumi explained. "All we can do is keep the team updated and let Je-hu know what's going on with the committee," Tumi added with enthusiasm.

"What we don't need is the committee to find our members and dispose of our opposition before the campaign starts," Sora exclaimed.

"They may need to be held at a new meeting place so they are guarded heavily by the Malaysia we have held up there. Let's bring them together and let them know it is the safest place for them at this time. I don't think there will be any argument from them," Tumi exclaimed getting up to leave.

They both set out to get the members and make them safe.

Chapter 21

Tumi started reading; "Intez," Born: Wing Hospital, twenty-five rotations past (.0025)

Resides: Ysolda
Holds office: District, Pazar Est.

I want to do this solo with little as possible, or no baggage. Rox is far Tumi has to plan for a cross-continent after getting off the Island. Going south has a few vegetation and wildlife dangers to consider. Starting with Red Ire, they have very few enemies, mainly because they are so small.

Or so it seems. They travel in packs between the numbers of four and ten. When they begin ingestion of their victim they become very large, by that, I mean to say they grow in proportion to the amount they have consumed. Their size starts out the size of your fingernail and they, after ingesting their prey, can become the size of your whole hand.

In that stage of digestion Ire's are neutral. They can be easily overtaken and destroyed. The hardest danger to get past is scabies, these are little beings that are similar to pygmies but smaller and more dangerous. Because they hibernate it's hard to know when and where they will show up. They are primitive hunters and use crude weaponry but it is effective for killing and they are vicious.

The teeth on these creatures are small and arrowhead shaped, facing inward, so when they take a bite they don't let go. They have to be ripped off of your body taking a piece of flesh with them. They only stand about one foot high so the piece taken is severe enough to cause heavy bleeding and leave a blood trail that keeps them coming back or cause a major infection that can leave you weak or dead.

Then they, scabies, come and drag the victim back to their domain and devour it. There are also some predators that scare the hell out of Tumi. Even with an immune booster, he would still have a problem with parasites and flying carnivores.

One of the largest flying creatures in the region he is to be travelling in, called Zyu, has a wingspan of ten feet. It can carry two Quaians at one time, it's unusual to happen but it does. Even with a platform it can overtake him and carry him off.

Females are the most likely to do this during hatching periods. Dracos are also feared these are land beasts but can pounce with winged accuracy. They don't fly as their wings are too short to keep their massive bodies in the air. But they allow these creatures to glide for distances of up to seven feet giving them a chance to accurately subdue their prey.

These creatures are territorial and live only in certain regions of Kranqus. Tumi has to pass through one of these regions in order to find two of the candidates, so preparation is vital, camouflage is the safest and the best way to travel.

It took Tumi three days to find what he needed before he could go, now he can feel safer but it's a false sense of safety. But for the idea of it, he is ready, ready to challenge the region's dangers. Grabbing his travel bag he steps onto the flat board and takes off. These new forms of travel are smooth, it's like surfing the air, with easier manoeuvrability until approaching multiple obstacles then it can be a dangerous ride at high speeds.

Moving at one hundred feet above the ground, he sees everything and his direction is a simple observation. His first on the list is "Samar."

Born: Quirec Outreach, thirty-eight rotations past (oo38)
Resides: Quirec north, Sub Qui
Holds office: Sub-district of Qui north

Samar is not new to adversity he has been a part of a group known as Society for Political Democracy or (SPD) and Tumi wants to get this done, so it's known who is working the candidacy, we need three if all agree to be a part of this intervention that would be an optimistic approach there would be a back up to each one of the candidates, observation and advisors. It would be a progressive team and would ensure a win by at least one of the three leaders. We are hoping for a first-time female elected.

This would ensure true change and a committee overthrow, Naveen, if she doesn't know it now, she has the most important role, and she will learn this as we bring everyone together in the next few weeks. Samar has the safest route, living in one of the highest regions of Kranaqus It's far but that means he can work his way into Rox from there. He set off; the first day was easy with nothing compromising the time, on the second day a storm came in from nowhere, that's just how it is with winds blowing in from the mountains.

Finding shelter wasn't easy, so he hung a hammock from a tree branch, this is the best way when dealing with sudden storms though there is a lot of rocking and hopeful thinking that the branch won't break at any time hurling you down to the ground a fall that could easily kill you or seriously injure a person. When he awoke the storm was still going on, less intense but raining.

By using the platform Tumi is avoiding a few perils and dangerous creatures that roam the forests of Kranaqus something that Naveen hadn't considered, as he passed her on his second day's travel. Not observing any movement in the camp, he assumed she was still sleeping.

The second day was just as uninterrupted but he noticed, in the distance a dark flying creature, and thought to avoid it. So he lowered the platform and decided to fly at tree level. Knowing that tall plant life is spaced in clusters and sparsely routed, leaving open ground between each grouping. Even while in the open area he still felt safer as he flew between dispersed clusters of forests.

Not knowing that, just above him and a little to the left, so the shadow is not noticed, it is ready to make its move. The breeze felt good on his face and he knew exactly how he's going to approach Samar, and then it happened. All he could feel is the tightness around his shoulders, it wasn't painful but he couldn't combat the grip and the more he struggled the tighter it grew to be. Now he was being taken in a different direction and there was nothing to do but allow it to happen, for the time being.

Tumi realised that he is being taken east to a higher altitude. It was too far and too high, the talons were not hurting him or penetrating his skin but he knew that this flight could only last a short time before he learned what he is about to become. Food, and there it was, they were three heads in a cave shelter on the side of a cliff, their long necks stretching out awaiting for dad to bring in the nourishment, three Zyu's, pray is always fed life or it will not be accepted by the young.

Tumi had to think and act fast or this quest is over for him. The platform he is on is powerful, but just how much power does it have? Tumi gets an idea. By flipping upside down and reversing the power from the bottom to the top, giving a magnetic surge from the top flat board and keeping the bottom at a low variable, while upside down, Tumi can propel a blow under the breastplate of the creature and knock the breath out of it, as well as force the Zyu up into the atmosphere, where the air is thinner.

This will render the Zyu unconscious loosening the grip around Tumi's shoulders so he can make good his escape and then let the creature drop to the ground, killing it. As he got closer to the cliff the Zyu started to focus more on flapping, to stay atop the opening where the hatchlings are. With each upward flap, he loosened his grip. Tumi took the moment and acted.

Watching it fall he began contemplating the moment. What was a Zyu doing up here? These creatures almost never roost above 30,000 feet. Tumi is up at 79,000 where the air starts getting thinner than most creatures can tolerate and it becomes difficult to breathe and maintain responsiveness. Tumi got back into form and headed, as quickly as possible, to Quirec. Not wanting to encounter more surprises he did the rest of the journey without rest and began looking for the residence of Samar.

Finding it he discovered Samar was not there, what to do? Finding his office might be an all-day search, so he opted to stay and wait, make something to eat, as he hadn't eaten since the attack, he waited. While lying about he got the idea to post a message on the front door to give Samar a moment of pause and time for Tumi to make his entrance.

Upon his approach, Tumi got as close as Samar's walk to the front door and was stopped by two hooded guards. They began redirecting him towards a waiting caged platform when Samar stepped out from behind the front door.

"Wait," he hailed. The guards turned and escorted Tumi to Samar who was waiting at the front door of his home.

"It's a good thing you posted the message on my front door the way you did or you would be halfway to the questioning halls right now," Samar said motioning him inside, and went on to say, "you wouldn't want to be confronted by the members of that place, they begin with ripping off your fingernails before asking questions."

Samar started putting together a hot beverage and, while motioning to join him with a cup he asked, "What is it I can help you with?" after accepting the cup he began, “You are well known for your outspoken contempt against the comity. I have a proposition for you and if I can have a few hours of your time today I would like to explain what it is and leave you to make your decision.”

“Yes, I have the rest of the day to myself and can give you as much time as you need, anything making change possible so Kronos can have a better representation of government is worth making time for.” Tumi began by saying, and went on to explain in detail.

After three hours, they shook hands and Tumi departed with a positive feeling and knowledge that Samar is going to be at the meeting in the next three weeks.

“Now onto number two,” he thought to himself, as he contemplated the dangers. Dracos are creatures that stock their prey, they don’t attack until they are sure they are not detected then pounce, silently, from above.

Jyati: born Gwennole
Alive for (oo35) rotations
Resides Wing
Holds office, wing east, a suburb community.

Tumi got to Gwennole without incident, although he did see the occasional dracos and zyu, they were already preoccupied with other captures so getting to Gwennole was uncompromised by the incident. Arriving was the usual, getting set at a dwelling, purchasing a map and seeking the residence. Upon doing so he discovered an unexpected curiosity.

There was heavy security around the premises and citizens, from what it looked like could only be perceived as are mourners. So Tumi went up and asked, “What is happening that there is so much sadness?”

The security guard replied, “Jyati was out hunting over the past several days and met an ill-fated circumstance.”

“Oh, what was it, if I may be so bold,” said Tumi continuing with his inquiry.

“He, unfortunately, was being stalked by a Dracos, and before anything could be done to elude it, it attacked and carried him off to who knows where,” “holy Ire, I believe I know where, I passed a Dracos feasting on my way into town, It’s not more than ten miles away.” pointing in a Northern direction.

"Well, then," looking in the direction Tumi was pointing, "I'll go and let the family know so they can gather and go find the location. Can you take them back to it if they require assistance," asked the guard.

"Yes, as I said. It's not far from the town and easy to find when can they be ready?" Tumi asked looking at the house and the family standing around the front entrance.

"Let's go and enquirer and I can introduce you to the family and make arrangements to find where you saw this Dracos." He is leading Tumi into the house.

He introduced him to the grandfather and they sat and talked about the location and made arrangements to go there in the morning. Tumi left and went back to his accommodation and waited till the morning to show the location.

Upon their arrival to where the body lay the identification was made and they brought the body back to the town to prepare him for burial. Tumi decided not to stay, as he had business elsewhere and it could not wait. So he was off to Winog.

Winog, being so close, was only a half-day on the board, and when he got there was surprised by the Zyus flying overhead. The citizens were running wild trying to avoid being victimised by swooping and diving Zyus. In the few minutes he arrived he watched ten being carried away. It was like a feeling of delirium, but from above rather than in the field of ravenous beasts.

Tumi was on the other side of the town so, far from the carnage. When he felt it was over he slowly crept into the streets and looked for a place of accommodation. Tumi sat down on the side of his bed and began thinking how just with a half day's travel, into another region, wildlife is completely different. But that's how this township got its name, because of the high population of Zyu in the area, it was named Wing, and the only reason it has such a high population of citizens is its resources.

There are many minerals gems and sand, to make glass. Mineral mixtures, makes some of the best glass, coming from this region, creating the element of necessity, and a place to make large amounts of remuneration. The reason there is such a high population of Zyu is, there are always two suns on this side of the planet, as one is a constant fixture in this southern polarity giving it a constant temp of twenty-eight degrees Celsius.

Tumi, after finding a tavern with accommodation, began to settle in and prepared to go seek a map to find Intez residence and office. After eating he found a map at the local curator and went back to his room to go over the best way to his residence. He then crashed to wait for the next day's end.

The next morning, after a meal, he decided to go to Intezs office just to introduce himself and arrange to meet back at his Intezs residence. As he entered his office he introduced himself and waited for the acknowledgement from Intez. Instead, he received a different name, "Hi, I'm Jayuntai. If you are looking for Intez, I'm afraid you're too late. The Zyu are on the wing and have been for a couple of weeks, there was no warning and it's unusual to have swarms at this time, but something has changed and things are very different this season.

"Anyway, Intez was attacked right outside his residence, it was so fast, no one could do anything, he didn't have a chance. So I've stepped in to replace him until the next election."

"Oh, then I guess what I came for is mute and I'll return to Rox today, thanx," and Tumi left the building to return to his accommodation and prepare for his return to Rox.

Chapter 22
Believe

As you come to know
What it is that you miss
In the days that follow
The moments are dismissed
There are no endings
The only thing that's pending
Is the kiss

We wonder
And ponder taking
Change by the alter
Another day
Has just gone by
Another year
Between you and I

As the world thirsts
The night skies envelope
As we all succumb
To what's now
Or what's yearning
What we find is
Tomorrow takes it's turn

As the flowers bloom
And as the birds sing
In springs light
There is something new
Bringing new life in
Making time right
Seeing and believing too

As I do believe in you

Je-hu, sat in his chair and began contemplating his route, and thought to himself, "Now, who can I bring into the mix, to take my place, Nayrr."

He knew though if he wanted it done right, doing it himself is the only way. He also knew the dangers of each area he was heading into. Encarta's are beautiful when in full bloom, and are not to be feared, you have to step onto them before it can harm you, it's more the flying creatures, the crawling creatures, and beasts small and large that I am not familiar with so I must do this in haste as time is limited and the dangers are not my strong point of knowledge.

As I am travelling into unknown territory an immune booster is relevant, this will fight some of the unknowns. By that I mean, this is a hostile time of evolution and my immune system is from a more temperate time, so some of the viruses, poisons from creatures crawling and flying are not known and I have little or no defences against them. If I had grown up in this environment my immunity would be stronger.

But I haven't so this booster is necessary. I will also be using a levitation platform, it will make the journey longer than jumping, but faster than depending on beasts or walking, lighter because I will depend on much less and simpler.

Even though the two are extreme distances apart, the platform will make it in days rather than weeks. But I can also stream and be finished in a few days, as well, and wait for the arrival of all the accepting candidates. Going over the first folder "Esyr" I can see he has three terms in his district, this is good, he has enough experience to know what he is in for and not enough to pose a threat to the comity until it's too late.

He is liked by the populous, or he wouldn't have been re-elected. So, I will approach him after "Lymad". He is very new to his political seat, only serving for two years in his district. So, Lymad will be first. Lymad is in one of the smaller ridings in Gwennole, south of Rox, if I jump I can have him interviewed and he can make the decision in the next few days.

Although he is politically new, he has already voiced contempt at the comity, which is unusual because most newbies are more likely to please rather than create friction. So I'll jump tomorrow and approach him at his residence before he goes to his head office.

Because he had been in this area before he knew where he could jump without being observed, upon jumping his walk would be at least two hours. So, he jumped early. As he entered the yard, through the window, he could see someone sitting at a table. Assuming it is Lymad he knocked on the door.

Getting up, Lymad took a sip from his beverage and walked to the door, opening it, he looked at the figure standing in front of him.

"It's a little early for visitations. What can I do for you?" Lymad asked.

Introducing himself Je-hu said, "Good day, my name is Je-hu might I come in, I have something to discuss of great importance, concerning the election to be announced in the next few weeks."

Lymad gestured to enter; Je-hu did so and seated himself at the table.

“I am an ambassador from Rox and have been sent to find candidates for the election, to become Emperor, and you are among the chosen, one of seven, to be interviewed. Are you able to spend some time right now to discuss your candidacy or participation with our members?”

Lymad offered a hot beverage and began with “You came on the right day, as it turns out, I don’t have to be in until this afternoon, so, I’ll give you two hours, that way I still have some downtime before leaving.”

After an hour and a half of explanation Je-hu shook hands and left, Lymad poured another cup and began contemplating what he heard with serious supposition. Je-hu walked towards a forested area to make his second jump, he had not secured a platform and had to rely on the area map he obtained. The frustrating consideration is that Je-hu is taking the chance because, in the area where Esyr lives there are sand parasites that prey on any land being, and sand parasites, after consuming their sustenance, go into hibernation for two months and emerge as winged kinenchi, these creatures are very unpredictable.

They can appear completely non-aggressive, because they already have their victim, and are satisfied being voracious in appetite they need to eat every hour. Their life cycle is five days, and then have to spawn, depending on the climate of the season, the cooler the season the longer the cycle, the warmer the season the shorter the cycle. The only way to safeguard yourself from them is to rub the root of the Encarta on your skin.

This will keep the kinenchi from injecting the venom, causing paralysis and suspension of body function, so it can suck the fluids and later go back and continue to inoculate its victim with eggs. That is why wire mesh is so important on any trek to the outer regions on this planet, these flying parasites are everywhere, they have different cycles but similar ways of metabolising their young.

Je-hu needs to find a different way of transport and a platform is the ultimate; it’s fast and can carry a load. So he started looking at different buildings. The only ones that would possess a craft such as this is municipal being that they always have the latest updated resources to make their work faster and more accessible and efficient. Going into the library he happened to see one in the far corner of the room.

These are huge rooms with eighteen-foot-tall bookshelves, so it is necessary to have at least one, but this place had two. Now to devise a way to take one without suspicion or notice until it was too late. First to gather some equipment, necessary for the trip a tent, camping stove, cooking supplies, and a few other things, it took most of the day but he was ready before closing. So Je-hu went inside the building and found a place to hold up where it would be hard to detect while the management was closing.

After an hour, when he was sure no one was in the building he emerged, finding the platform he wanted exiting is now the issue. Without jumping how could he do this? Pondering this thought he remembered the funnels at the top of the peak, ventilation, but the platform is too wide. So Je-hu began removing the trim for the extra space he would need to pull it through, he will have to turn it from corner to corner.

By turning it on, it will maintain a pulse and be easy to manoeuvre through the vent main. The only thing is the time to put it all back together with no tools. So he proceeded to pound the trim together with his fist, it worked but it was sloppy. Je-hu stepped onto the platform flew over to where he stashed his equipment and took off towards Esyr.

Parasites

Swarms:

While Ohn-ohn was alive he told me of a season of swarm storms, in some regions that inflict strange and terrifying disastrous disappearances, sometimes losing whole villages and townships. One day, they are there and you have walked through a lively thriving population the next time you wander into that district there is nothing, no shelter, no stables, no farms, no people, no life, no town, nothing.

How does this happen? Storms can be and are severe, but there is always debris scattered around to show what was, especially in the worst-case scenarios. When there is nothing to find it is a very suspicious and eerie encounter to find. Some places are void of life for a reason that is not always known.

The dark cloud formed a tornado funnel that touched the ground as it swirled in a counter clockwise rotation there was no dust, so it had no high winds but more of a sweeping motion that seemed deliberate, it would sometimes have a central bulge that would then break showing a gap and then re-join after a few seconds.

This was peculiar because in violent storms everything happening in the vortex is always connected ad inseparable with volumes of dust and debris flying off and being carried into the tube, where it would be torn apart or thrown into another region of the province. There were no overhanging clouds just the tube-like tornado, Je-hu wondered if he should move in closer to see what he was witnessing, but thought better of it. Yet it was right in the path of where he was heading.

Esyr lives just on the edge of the desert along the river of Aza in the township of Bombyx. This town is so named because it has manufacturing of a material produced by a butterfly that makes silk. This material can only be produced in this area because of the dryness of the region.

These butterflies can only exist in this area where a certain plant called a cactus spike flower that can only grow in sandy regions with freshwater runoff, of which there are only two known one on the border of Kranaqus and Akir, and the other inside Zed. And he is on his way to Bombyx, where Esyr holds the largest riding for that municipality, and where the kinenchi are most denizens.

He decided to go around, a good decision he felt, as it would eliminate the inconvenience of injury or something more severe such as death. It only took an extra half-day to go around and the funnel didn't move, so it is what he suspected a swarming storm, and they must have had something in their feeding grasp because it formed middle bulges that swooped to the ground every so often.

Upon arriving in Bombyx, Je-hu looked for a place of accommodation. After getting settled into a place, outside the villages district to maintain discretion, he then found a correspondence shop to retrieve a map, upon doing so he also browsed through a market and bought some food for the preparation of dinner, feeling he would be here for a couple of days, he bought enough for a few days, thinking that it would save him some money and keep him on a more discreet path.

After eating he poured himself a drink, to relax, while he went over the map in search of Esyrs residence. All residence in every municipality, large or small, especially when holding office, or running a large or small industry and business, is mapped. In this way all people are known in rural and urban areas, even outside the populated areas will have a mapping of roads, trails for walking and driving, all vehicles are either pulled by beasts or electrically charged motors.

There are no combustible fuels used for propulsion, everything is electrically charged other than for weaponry, fires, when out in forested regions and meadows, where one is isolated it is used for the purpose of keeping away beasts and creatures. Fuels are also used for lamps and cooking. Gases are also used in the same manner, not for propulsion. There has not been any motorised gas propulsion invented, as of yet, in this world.

The next day Je-hu got on his flat board to find Esyrs residence, it took a small part of the morning and as he assumed no one was home, so he resolved to return after business hours to interview Esyr, and went back to his accommodation to make a midday meal remaining indoors until the appropriate time to see Esyr.

Finding Esyrs residence he lowered his board and, seeing someone is home, went to knock on the door. Esyr answered after he did so and asked, "Hello, I can tell, you are not from around here, what is your purpose or are you expecting a hand-out?"

"No, not a hand-out, I have a proposition for you. I would like to come in and explain what it is." so Esyr motioned him to enter and they both went to the living area to converse. It took Je-hu almost three hours to go over the information and proposal before concluding with, "It is very important that we have you on board for this your knowledge and years in the office gives you an advantage over all the others we have selected."

Looking at him straight in the eyes Je-hu continued, "If you need some time to think it over I'll be here for a couple of days."

"No, I don't think I need it, I can answer you right now. How much time do I have to get my business in order?" Esyr said without hesitation.

"Three weeks. We need to bring everyone together so we can begin the process to know who will lead the campaign."

They both exchanged cards and Je-hu expressed his thanks and looking forward to seeing him in three weeks. Je-hu got on his board and went back to his accommodation then started packing for the journey back to Rox. He decided on the same route, it didn't appear to have any complications, as suggested by Tumi. Je-hu felt like waiting till the next day before setting off, so he prepared dinner and settled in for the late period with a good drink.

The next morning he headed back to Rox.

Chapter 23
Muse

One hundred malicious
Little mysteries
Ends up in
Some bodies fantasies
Someone else
To recognise
Yet in the end
It's based on lies

Be still the night
In REM
Trapped I find
In love again
Muse be free
In time you see
Trapped again
In REM

One hundred malicious
Little mysteries
Have entered into
My midnight sleep
Reflecting back
It cannot be
Still, I can't
Escape the dream

One hundred malicious
Little mysteries
Have entered into
Your midnight, sleep
Reflecting back
To recognise
And still, it comes out
Based on lies

Sit-in Fourteen

As they were seating themselves to begin the meeting "Where is Kaylex?" asked Fanyrottiss. "We need the info on each of our opposition subjects."

Just then Kaylex entered and set down, on the table, three folders each containing the histories of the candidates on the opposition.

"It took a bit of digging but I have compiled the backgrounds of each subject and included in their medical histories, it seems that there is nothing specific to consider except for where they all are from. Every candidate has lived above 15,000 kilometres above sea level which isn't suspicious on its face but brings to question, why?" exclaimed Kaylex.

"Well, it does give an element of mystery, but nothing to really consider dangerous or suspicious, it just leaves us with questionable intentions and what they are leading up to. What I think would be helpful is to bring one of them in for questioning, then we would have the upper hand, and direct our attack at the source of the conspirators," said Fanyrottiss.

"And whom might that be?" asked Axyon.

"That's what we need one of the conspirators for, once we know what we're up against we can eliminate this ghost and end all compromising circumstances, and resume our business in the usual order. But until then we tread lightly," Kaylex said with a stern tone looking at all the board members.

"Bobal is supposed to be here as well," just then a face peered around the threshold of the door; Babol entered the room and sat at the table. Looking around he noticed they were all focused on him.

"I guess you're waiting for an update," he questioned.

"Yes, that would be a good start," Axyon replied looking down at the papers in front of him.

"Well, as you know we've been searching throughout the different regions and found nothing, so we have concluded that Hazatt is on one of the islands of Xyph. This you already know there are no trails or roads on the islands so they are very difficult to negotiate all the islands in a reasonable time. I have two hundred men covering the four larger islands and after they are finished with them they will tackle the smaller ones."

Bobal continued, "We cannot know how long it will take or if he will be found at all, the bigger Islands have many caves and the natives are not cooperative with outsiders especially when confronted by soldiers from Rox," he said looking about the table.

“That’s not surprising,” said Fanyrottiss, “we will take this up again at a later date, but right now we have a more serious matter at hand.” Fanyrottiss looking around the room continued, “Axyon.”

Chapter 24
If I Say Yes

Death
I know where you are
You can't hide
From me

Death
I know who you are
Your not always
Who you seem

Yes
I don't wish upon stars
It's not always
What it seems

If I say yes
What does it mean
Does it come with a smile
Or part of the dream

If I say no
Who do you see
Can there be surmise
Or a probability

When Je-hu, Naveen, and Tumi arrived, the members of the opposition were waiting at the entrance to the meeting place. The meeting place is a cave outside the town of Xylem, the candidates were standing outside, questioning if they were in the right place. Je-hu arrived first and brought them deep into the cave, there they saw the staging of infiltration tactics that they are to learn over the next four weeks.

As Tumi and Naveen showed, Samar asked, "What's this game board?"

Je-hu answered, "I'm glad you asked; this game is something you will learn as we go into the debates it will help with a brain thought patterns, and strategies. It has been proven that it enhances brain function and ideas. But before we get into this we will find who is working with whom. "Looking at each of them and going over their positions of office and what they represented to get elected to the position they hold at this time.

"How do we do this." he thought aloud." he thought aloud. "Yes, what we can do is stick to the individual's discovery, so Naveen is with Zavita, Tumi is with Samar, and I will take Esyr. Does everyone agree?"

They all nodded.

And Je-hu went on to say "I have handed in the paperwork early and this is what I have outlined. Tumi and Samar will discuss libertarian, Naveen and Zavita will lead a social discussion, Esyr and I will argue a conservative strategy. We have only four weeks to pull this together, I want to see you all back here next week same time with at least a start on your openings. You all must have an idea of what you are and how to lead each discussion.

"The committee is cunning and sly and will know or begin to figure out a conspiracy, it is up to us to create diversion and obfuscation. We will adjourn this meeting until next week go home and get settled in. thank you all for showing up with such enthusiasm, I'll see you next week."

They all left and, taking their candidates, went home to settle them in and get acquainted with each other.

Je-hu, on the other hand, because he had no place to stay, took Esyr to a nearby tavern and entered him in for a few nights to keep him in sight and in a place close to the meeting place. His concern was being seen, if he wandered too deep into he stood the chance of becoming known, so he left Esyr on his own while he got comfortable.

They all went through the week working on their opening speeches remaining indoors for most of the time, this made being discreet more probable so they could bring a better presentation.

The week went by quickly and when Je-hu arrived they were all waiting at the entrance except one "Where's Esyr," asked Je-hu.

"We thought he would show up with you," they all said at once.

"We must find him, when I went to the tavern where he was staying he wasn't there. I'm going to assume we've been discovered, so the best source would be

Misric, he was saved by Naveen and Tumi and is a committee member. Where have you got him to hold up?" he asked looking at Naveen.

"He's at a place of my childhood, I used to go there to play with my brother and sister, and they are the caves off the shores of Kaya district where the land of Xyph is closest. It will take at least two days to get there to retrieve him and the same to return, If I leave now I can be back in four or five days and we can get some answers. We must act swiftly, it has already been a week and we don't know what the committee may have learned or done to Esyr," Naveen said with great urgency.

"We have to change our meeting place, Tumi, do you know of any other place close by that can act as a temporary accommodation?" asked Je-hu.

"Yes, Lake CRC has an underground cavern accessible from the hills surrounding the western shores ten kilometres before the lake. The entrance is difficult so it's best we meet in the field before the tree line into the hills," Tumi suggested.

"Hey, Lake CRC, the area you're referring to is on the south side of Xylem is it not," said Naveen.

"That's right, from the meadow I can take you to the entrance," Tumi exclaimed.

"Go Naveen, take Tumi, we'll all meet there in six days," Je-hu replied, and gestured the others inside.

After they all got settled Je-hu continued, "What have you all accomplished? I would like to know or hear your opening rhetoric let's start with Zavita."

As they spent the rest of the day going over their introductions and speeches Naveen prepared to leave for the caves of Kaya.

Naveen realised that she would be going to pick up Misric and would not need anything but food and extra clothing, so she prepared a small travel pack and went over to Tumi's to ready themselves to leave. Tumi was already packed and waiting, getting on his flat board and they both headed off to the caves.

They reached the caves in two days without incident and found Misric in a state of distress and frustration.

"I didn't know if you were ever coming back for me" he snapped, "I've been chained here for three days now and I'm running out of water and food. This isn't right. I'm a member of the high council and demand better quarters and proper food."

“You be thankful that you’re even alive remember how you were brought here in the first place. You were about to be beheaded if you can recall and this is the safest and best place for you right now,” Naveen said in a smooth tone. “If we hadn’t been there you would be under the ground rather than above it, so I suggest you calm down and cooperate with us or we will release you to the dogs after we are done with you.”

“Well, it’s good to see that I haven’t been forgotten and left to rot. What are you planning anyway?”

“We have the need for you in Kranaqus, there has been an incident and we need your knowledge.” Naveen went on, “someone is missing and we need to know what has happened to him, where he might be taken, and if he is still alive,” Naveen said staring him in the eyes.

“Well,” Misric replied, “if he is taken by the council he is surely dead, or on the edge of it. They will keep him alive only to find out what they need to know and then he will inevitably be killed.”

“Then we don’t have much time and need to return now,” said Tumi.

Unchaining Misric from the wall, they put him on his own platform and chained him to it, with a tether attached to Naveen’s, so Tumi was free to act if Misric tried to escape. It will take them three days to return to Rox and the new meeting place because they are starting late in the day.

As they started off they looked at each other and realised they could stay along the shoreline of the ocean and avoid most of the hazards and predators lurking in the forested areas, it will also cut some of the time, but only by a few hours, these flat boards can only do fifty or sixty kph. There first few hours went smooth because they could stay close to the shoreline but as they get closer to the cliffs of thunder brake the waters become more treacherous and the terrain becomes mountainous. So they will have to make some decisions about what path they want to travel.

They spent the night at the foot of the cliffs, just before the beaches end, they made it as comfortable as possible with tree branches and found as big a sandy area as the rocky shore line would provide. It was more of resting than sleep but at least they could eat something and observe what the weather is going to be like.

In this part of the continent, storms can erupt unexpectedly and if you caught on the surf the waves can get so large that they engulf you swallowing up everything, dragging them under, or smashing it onto the cliff's edge. This they want to avoid, so heading into the mountains is the only alternative.

Getting to the top of the cliff was not the problem; the flat boards took them easily, governing their way across the upper plains was also not a problem nor was the narrow passages that led to the deep caverns, the problem was the Zyus seen over the mountains as they reached the first drop, into the valley of darkness, this is just a metaphor because there is no night on any of the planet's darkness can only occur in caves, caverns, and deep holes.

It can also be created, different structures can be made dark, and when making below ground foundations, they can be dug hundreds of metres deep, and be made into living quarters, as well as offices, and keeping storage.

The valley of darkness is named that due to heavy swarming red Ires are not the only insects or parasites that swarm, there are many and the dark valleys is the most notorious for this event there are three in the region Naveen, and Tumi are headed. Swarming has no season it can happen at any time of every rotation, and there are three to cross. There is a great chance that one of them has a swarm.

Not all swarms are deadly but darkness is, there are ghosts. What is meant by that is plants, animals, and insects can't be seen and can attack, sting, or reach out and scratch anyone passing by causing death or extreme illness. These happenings are referred to as ghost encounters, as they are usually unexplainable.

They stopped at the edge of the high cliff to observe the surrounding first valley, "Do you see it?" asked Naveen pointing towards the south and into the second valley.

"Yes," answered both in unison.

"We need to avoid that area for sure, but all that means is there are probably more scattered throughout that whole region. So, I suggest we stay as close to the water as possible." Naveen made a gesture towards the west and they all saw the black clouds forming over the ocean. Storms can create a form of darkness, but there is always enough light to govern one's way through most environments, but the storms are violent.

"I'd rather chance the storm than a swarm," said Misric.

"Well, it looks like we made the wrong decision with sticking to the coast, so suggest we go down this first valley and valley take the original route back to Rox," Tumi stated pointing out a new trail that from their location looked easy and more approachable.

"The power on our boards is draining, we need to be back in Rox in two days, if we take this route it will be possible if there are no other compromising situations in our path." Naveen pointing to the swarm in the second valley, "that could easily move into our direction without warning so let's be aware of where it is and where we are."

She began down the hillside and, though Misric was tethered to Naveen they were all still able to spread out to avoid entanglement staying above the tree line and giving a clear observation of the second valley and the swarm.

Entering the lower forest and leaving the valley they headed towards Ockuyu, they all know this trail well and found it nonthreatening. Arriving in Rox a few hours before the meeting Naveen took Misric to where they are to meet and chained Misric to the floor, making sure it was sound and firm. She then went back to her place and prepared for the meeting getting into some fresh clothes after showering and made something to eat.

Tumi, upon arriving at Rox, Tumi went straight to his suit, showered and changed, then, after eating a quick snack, sought out to find Je-hu.

Chapter 25
It's Funny

Once in a memory
Or was it make believe
As in a misery
We practice deceiving

Sometimes you sit in wonder
Or does time condescend
Somewhere there's a fortune
But the rainbows
Never end

Something is burning
As we walk through the hall
Someone is yearning
To come unto you

Finding the meaning
In the books, they lay
Finding the reasons
Against the waves

Once in a fantasy
Time does condescend
Somewhere there's a fortune
But the rainbows never end

It's funny you know
How things come and go
Like a snowfall
On a sunny day
Wonderful the feeling
A moment's breeze
And knowing
Tomorrow is yesterday away

Sit-in Fifteen

"What have we discovered, about our new team of conspirators," as Fanayrotiss sat at the table expecting something extreme.

"Well," started Hazatt we have a surprise for you in holding, I think you'll like it." So they all got up and started down to holding, on the way Hazatt began how he had sent out a team to observe anything suspicious and will my men were sitting in a tavern in came two, out of the look of the territory, so when the one registered we took note at what suit they gave at the desk and found it to be right beside mine how coincidental, so after the second left the first stayed behind and while he was getting settled in we nabbed him.

"And here he is."

In the centre of the room sat a figure tied to a chair and blindfolded.

"He's in the state of stasis from the powder," said Hazatt, but as you know he can still understand and acknowledge what is being said and going on around him, so what I suggest is to let him know what information we want from him and he can think it through over the next few days, before coming out of the trance."

"Did you hear that? Blink if you understand."

Esyr blinked twice so they knew he was hearing them, and understanding what was going on, it would be at least two more days before the powder's effect would wear off, so until then the committee would have to wait. They all went back to the boardroom to discuss how they were going to handle the others on the opposition.

It was apparent they are not going to go away and, now that they had one in their possession whom they knew is going to die before the week's end, there is a forty per cent chance that one of them would take the seat of Emperor.

"How did you happen upon him," asked Fanayrotiss.

"It was purely by chance," Hazatt answered. "While one of Babols officers was in a tavern, outside the city, two citizens walked into the office looking for a place to stay. He overheard them talking, though he didn't know what they were referring to or what the conversation was about, they didn't look like they were from the area, so he decided to follow them and discover what room they were looking into.

"He thought they would be staying in the room together but seeing them separate that's when he took his chance to act. He thought the one that left would be his likely subject but he just disappeared. That's when he took the opportunity to grab the other one. He was just settling in and would not suspect anything especially being abducted."

Yasir and Ayxan had also come in with some startling news of their own. While doing an overall inspection of the Estate Ayxan found something that looked suspicious and in closer observation discovered a recording device. It was set in amongst a bunch of outdated technological devices and could have passed for junk, except it was still activated. They took the component and the disk it held and revealed that it had the last meetings info and all that went on in it.

Ayxan said excitedly, "It was found in the janitor's miscellaneous shelving, in their stockroom and storage. We have one of the two new recruits the other was killed trying to escape. It's obvious they are working together the other is in the lower dungeon he will be questioned severely and then put to death of course."

"Well, it appears, we have been compromised and the conspirators know everything to date. Resolving power is in order and that will come from the janitor if he talks."

Fanayrotiss expressed with intensity looking about the room "I guess we have two to question and hopefully there hasn't been anything we can't overcome. We have to assume that all past sit-ins have been compromised and the traitors know everything we discussed. We must find out before the beginning of the campaigning or we are done. We will be exposed to the people and anything planned will be a wash."

Fanayrotiss looked at Axyan and said firmly, "Go to the janitor and find out who sent him as well as how many spies are staffed here. There has to be more. Yasir, you will accompany him and find out anything in any way possible. He will be put to death so hold no restraint."

Axyan and Yasir departed and went down to the lower dungeon there they found the janitor dying from a self-inflicted wound. He had been put in a cell and chained but still had some mobility. There were extra rings tied into the walls with chains dangling from them.

Raju had made his way over to the closest one he could reach and, wrapping it around his throat, managed to tighten it enough to cut off the air and strangled himself.

"Red ire bastard" Axyan cried out he punched him in the face and began brutalising his body he turned to Yasir "get this piece of crap out of here, put it in the hole it will make good feed for the carnivorous down there."

“Well, I guess that kills anything we could have known from him,” Yasir said in relief.

Chapter 26
4/20

The grass
Lay on my keys before me
Free form
Appeals to mind me
And any soul
Who cares to listen
The grass
May bring a sense of time

Some times
We can awaken
And find ourselves
Lost in thought
Now and then
We can discover
What we have
And who we are

We can take you
As high as your mind
Has made you
Feel how it holds
Your mind you
Free your soul
In its time
Feel the high

The grass
Lay on my keys before me
Free form appeals
To mind me
Now and then
We can discover
What we have
And who we are

Tumi started walking the stone streets of Rox, he headed to where he thought Je-hu would be hanging out before making his way to the new meeting place. But Je-hu was nowhere, what Tumi didn't know is that Je-hu had jumped back to Devi and was consulting with his superiors and updating them on the progress of the situation on Qua, within Kranaqus.

"What have you got to report, Hu?" asked the chief of the council.

The council likes to use the name Hu when questioning him it is less formal and puts everyone more at ease.

"We have had to change our meeting place for fear of discovery, one of the oppositions has been taken, I am waiting for the return of a party of streamers who have a committee member hold up in the caves outside of one of the districts in Kranaqus. I am hoping he can be rescued before anything tragic happens to him but from the history of this committee, it's unlikely. Misric, as he is known, will also be able to help with strategy so that overthrowing these tyrants and starting a new era of governing and a free state of affairs."

Je-hu continued, "There will also be a much easier placement of the towers so the building of the web will be smoother and with less or no impediment. Once we have our candidate on the Emperor's throne we will be working on the alliance of all states to ensure a successful placement of structure so the outer atmospheric WEB can begin construction."

He explained "Well, it sounds as though you have it all planned well to advantage us with this conundrum, so be on your way and inform us when you have achieved your objective. We have faith in your plan, and execution that we will not intervene unless an 'emergency response' is sent by you." the chief responded.

"I must leave hastily, my team is going to meet in a few hours and I'm not there," Je-hu gestured.

"Go then, you have much to be planning, peace be with you," the chief stood and gave the departure insignia.

He jumped landing on a beach just offshore of the second meeting place as he was walking towards the beachside of the rocky shoreline he spotted Tumi. Yelling to get his attention he stumbled onto a brush.

"Are you alright?" asked Tumi.

"Ya," Je-hu answered.

"I've been looking for you and I thought you'd be here but how could I have missed you, I've been all over this area and you were nowhere, but suddenly here you are, how could I have missed you?" Tumi said quizzically.

"As you can see I've been fighting my way through the heavy brush I saw you and waited until you were in earshot before calling," said Je-hu.

"Naveen is with Misric and they should be at the sight now," replied Tumi.

As they arrived all the team were together no one was talking and Naveen stood up and approached Je-hu.

"We all met in the town muse and found the place together, that way nobody would be left behind or get lost.

"On the way here we went over each of our objectives and presentations but I'm assuming that's not what we're here to discuss," she said objectively looking at each of them ending by staring right into Misrics eyes with intensity.

"Your committee has one of our candidates."

Je-hu said staring at him with discussion, "Where would they be keeping him and how long has he got to live?"

"How long has he been gone?" asked Misric.

"Five days," Naveen answered.

"That's not good; let me give you an insight into what he is facing. First, to get him without a struggle he is put into a suspended anatomical state. This is done by a rare powder extracted from the blowfish; its poison sack is dried and used as a form of toxin. By blowing it into the face of the victim, in just a few seconds it renders the citizen semi-consciousness like suspended animation, like the undead. Yet, would still be able to hear, and understand all that is going on around them. That's when the torture begins."

Misric stood looking at all of them in the face with unquestionable forethought. "This continues for three days. The victim is then set on a stainless-steel table, on their side, in a foetal position with their head facing their abdomen, and disembowelled. This is done just before coming out of this suspended state so the feeling begins to come back, but the vocal cords are still delayed. There is no blood, even though the unfortunate one is cut from anus to Adam's apple.

"After removing it, Adam's apple, from under the chin it is flicked across the table onto the floor, the whole time the one having this done is able to see all that is happening. The last thing, before dying, is watching the innards spill over the sheen of the contour and slowly dies. And when I say slowly, it takes a normal citizen about two and a half hours before succumbing to this extreme." They were all aghast and Naveen showed signs of tearing as did Zavita. "But your member is in a unique position."

"How so," Zavita interjected.

"They need him, for now," he said in a modest fashion, "to find you all." looking at them he managed a grimacing grin that reminded them just who they have in their presence and why he was kept alive in the first place.

“We can then only assume he is dead, you on the other hand are still alive, thanks to the quick thinking of Tumi, and Naveen.” Je-hu grabbed him by the throat and threw him into a desk, “Draw a map on its location.”

“Which one, there are several,” Misric questioned.

“The one most likely to be used, you and I know which one that is,” looking him straight in the eyes Je-hu said, “The Estate. You give the exact location in the estate, level, room corridors to enter by, and how many posted guards there might be.”

Misric started drawing and began explaining why there may not be as many guards as might be anticipated, “We have no reason to think that anyone would be questioning what goes on in the estate. So, why the need to heavily guard the lower holding cells, the bodies don’t leave the lower levels there are deep pits designed to swallow any and all compromising or questionable deaths that occur in the dark interiors of the estate.”

Looking at what Misric was drawing Je-hu began explaining, “I also want the depth of each level, the location of the estate in the city, all the different devices in the room in which he would be held and what, if any, animal guards would be in the room. An exterior top view of the grounds and buildings, with sentry posts, and sight walking times,” demanded Je-hu.

“I don’t care how long it takes, just get it done.”

Je-hu turned to Naveen, “Watch him, you know the city and are more familiar with the area than most of them being you are or have been in the medical field serving the city and outside regions, you’ll know if he is deceiving us, and he knows the consequences. Your committee thinks you’re dead, don’t be a fool you have no allies, no one is looking for you, and you have no family.

“We’ve researched all of you on the committee and know what you have and how much you have to lose, your cooperation with us is all you have going for you now. Do the right thing and we all may get out of this in one piece and winners.” Je-hu looked around at all of them, “We are not in this to lose or to die, change must happen if we are to save this world.”

Chapter 27
The Interrogation

Necro Feel Yah

Squares are numbers
Numbered squares
Roll the next into
Centre stage
Paint by numbers
Acrylic made
It's plain to see
No one remains

Toying with hell
One pill at a time
Wishes to wells
Pennies to dimes
All for one
One for All
What it stands for
No one knows

Squares are numbers
Numbered squares
Roll the next into
Centre stage
What it stands for
No one cares

Necro feel yah
Necro love
Let me touch
What gods have loved
Sometimes somethings
Hurt the one's we love
Necro feel yah
Necro love

The three remaining members stood around Samar and waited for him to revive, it had been four days since his abduction, and they were getting impatient. The others, of the opposition, would have discovered he is missing and would probably have taken immediate action to prevent more compromises in their efforts to assume the Emperor's throne. They started discussing amongst each other just how they would get the location of where they are holding up, and whether they should kill him or keep him for barter.

"Do we want to start with cutting off his fingers?"

Harour sneered toying with them and tapping the instrument with the other.

"No," Fanyrottiss said with reluctance, "we cannot mutilate him, if we need him for trading off or as an exchange for any purpose he cannot appear mangled."

He slapped him, and putting his face right into Esyrs face, he asked, "Are you coherent?"

Samar nodded looking a little sluggish and appearing somewhat intimidated but said nothing.

"Get me the book, and the block, along with the five pounder," Ayxan walked over to the shelf in the far corner and picked out three pieces.

One, a thick book, about four inches thick, the other a four-by-four block of hardwood, and last a hammer Fanyrottiss referred to as the five pounders. Placing the items on the table next to Samar, Fanyrottiss then picked up the book, stepped back and slammed it down on the top of Esyr head. Stunned and hurting Samar stared straight at him and growled.

"That's not going to win you any metals," Fanyrottiss sneered.

"The only way you're going to get out of this alive is if you cooperate," he said placing the book on his torso.

He motioned to Ayxan to hold it while reaching for the hammer, and in one motion slammed it into the book. It knocked the wind out of him and it felt like being hit by a two by four. Fanyrottiss did it six more times and then stood back. Samar was slumped over trying to catch his breath, just as Axyan slammed him in the back. Surprisingly it didn't hurt much and helped him to gasp in a lung full and brought him into a more conscious state.

"Where do you meet?" demanded Harour "We know there are more of you," and he showed the papers of application for election. They only showed the names of the members, with no place of residence. That was only an option when applying, the applicant only had to put his office of position along with his name, that way they remain discreet and would make it harder to target them for abduction or assassination.

"How did you find me?" Samar whispered.

"It was by chance," said Axyan.

"One of our lieutenants was in the bar when you and the one you were with admitted you into a room. Who was that other?" he demanded. "Is he the one we need to talk to?"

Fanyrottiss stuck his fingers into Samar's eye sockets and pulled his head back, "Is he the one directing this conspiracy?"

"Conspiracy," Samar gasped, "is not all elections open to anyone holding office?" he said looking around at the three standing around him. Just then he felt a thwack on the side of his head stunning him for a moment, "obviously not."

"We decide who runs for the Emperor's seat and who will be seated not some unknown Dracos who has no knowledge of protocol or procedure," exclaimed Harour as Axyan slammed him in the head with the book twice more. Stunned, and bent over he whispered, "I'm beginning to understand now why things have been done in the manner that they are. There are no boundaries for you all, are there?" he said trying his best to look up at them.

"Your elections are a joke, the rumours are all true. You mislead the public so you can remain in power. All the governing members have been talking, sending memos around of this conspiracy. Most did not believe it to be true. I was one of the disbelievers, but, as I sit here with the three of you, I am now convinced of what has been said and passed through the grapevine is true. You are all traitors..."

Just as the block slammed him in the shoulder knocking him to the floor Samar said, "Ires, all of you, you will all pay for your treachery."

"Enough of your sputum, where do you meet?" Fanyrottiss yelled angrily gritting his teeth.

"I would feed myself to a Zyu before giving up that information, I spit on you and your forefathers too." Samar verbalised as he lay on the floor trying to push himself up.

"You have disgraced yourselves and the Empire you, you supposedly represent, change is going to happen and you will be discovered."

Fanyrottiss, seething with anger, kicked Samar in the abdomen several times, and he, again fell to the floor.

"You all think you have it figured out, don't you." he gasped, "Where are the other two?" Samar questioned,

"There are five on the committee, how is it only three of you are standing here?" pulling himself up he looked up at them as best he could, "I'm sure they would be enjoying this as much as yourselves, what are they up to, or, when you revealed, will they be forever gone?"

"Enough of your questions, you are not here to ask anything, but to reveal the whereabouts of your demesne," exclaimed Fanyrottiss, with fists about his head.

"How long have I been gone? If it's been any length of days or weeks then they are already aware of my abduction, and would most likely have changed the location. So, my info would be of no help to you.

"What am I to expect? If I cooperate will I be spared or is this my finally and you're just keeping me around to use as a ploy to capture the rest of the applicants?" Samar stated as he lay about the floor not trying to move or appear unscathed by their relentless battery.

"No matter, though you are probably right, we want to explore the kind of space they would likely occupy so we can know what to look for. Also, things might have been left behind that could help with whom we are looking for. We have two more names, and we want them found before the campaign starts, that way there will be no question who is running and who will be seated," Fanyrottiss insisted.

"You don't know who they are or what they look like, do you. That's why you need me, isn't it." Samar turned on his back and passed out.

"What do we do with him now?" asked Harour.

"Strap him down on the table for now and let me know when he comes around, and we'll start all over again. If nothing comes of it, you know the drill." Fanyrottiss motioned his finger to his throat and swiped from ear to ear.

Chapter 28
The Decision

The Edge of Heaven

Could you might you
So sail a wall
Travelling life's corridors
Do you think we'll fall
We are what we do and
Only memories remain

Death is it or is it not
The lust of life that
Does not grow
Sublime the spirit
The urban soul

The corridors of life
Remain in memories
Can any mind say
Where reality lay
Living with or without
Yet within

What is sanity
And where does it dwell
On the edge of heaven
Or inside hell
What is forgiveness
When does it show
On the edge of a cliff
Or down below

After Naveen handed him the maps, reassuring him that they are accurate, except for the floor plans as she had not been inside the room to know its layout, everything is accurate. Je-hu walked outside and into the forested area surrounding the meeting place and vanished. He could only assume that what

Misric drew on the floor plan was correct and hadn't betrayed him with inaccuracy or deception.

He did his first jump to land in the garden behind the estate, where he was sure he would not be observed. Wrong, there was someone standing to his left, stunned by the light visual and maybe, hopefully, blinded as well. He walked out of sight and observation, jumped again and this time with the coordinates of the spatial relation provided by Misrics floor plan.

It is accurate, Je-hu materialised right where he coordinated his activity pawn. Looking around the room he realised that Misrics accuracy was incredible, everything is just how he placed them, including the table, where, to his dismay, Samar lay exposed in his disembowelled revealing. Sickened, he did not wait to be discovered and jumped immediately to the first coordinates of the jump and walked back to the camp where the team was still mulling over what to expect from the committee in regards to Samar, and what could be done to rescue him if that were a consideration.

Je-hu looked around at all of the faces in front of him, turning to Misric he said, and "Well, I guess your life is important to you; after all, the floor plan was well drawn and exact. You could have had me encounter a mob of guards or worse. But all in vain, Samar is not with us.

"They did as you said, and all we can do is mourn his loss and move on, but plans have changed. We are not going to let this go unavenged. Misric, you must know the Empire very well and as the archives building, there must be emergency exits all throughout it.

"You have done an excellent job on the layout of the building now include the hidden exits. We are not going to wait for the election, to find out who the people are going to elect to the throne.

"We are going to gather as many soldiers in the opposing states to overtake the empire. I'm sure we'll have no problem finding an army. Zed leaders have already expressed their disinterest with a show of force, opposing takeover, or cooperation to the committee," he said with conviction.

Walking over to Tumi, he continued, "Someone has to meet with the leaders of Zed and convince them to act. There is little time and the window is now, we have our informant, as reluctant as he may be he is in no position to negotiate or oppose us. Our ultimatum is his resolving power. Tumi I'm hoping you will volunteer to go meet with Zed and offer a place in this historic moment."

Je-hu put his hand on his shoulder and looked him straight in the eyes, "What shall I tell them?" Tumi asked with a puzzled look on his face.

"Tell them that they will be free of persecution and war, they will continue to have their own government with no threat of outside intervention. We would like to negotiate cooperation with state trade and technologies, and last, there will be a share in the wealth discovered when we have control. Samar, can you write up a document proposing all that I have stated and Tumi can present it to the president of Zed," said Je-hu.

"What if we don't get the answer we want, these are very distrusting times and they have had no alliance in the past with any other state and have managed to fend off a takeover from Kranaqus." Samar handed Je-hu the document for his approval before Tumi left to present it to Zeds leaders.

Approving what he had read he handed it to Tumi and said, "Be swift we have very little time and we need to know how we are going to pull this together. The flat boards are few and travelling by land would be observed, and we would lose any element of surprise. So, bring up the suggestion of meeting off the shores here."

Je-hu pointed at the new location to meet, "Also, we don't want an overwhelming number of group action. Therefore, five hundred volunteers would be the maximum to involve."

"You have the proposal go now, take a flat board; you will be a few days getting there and back upon your reply. Stay out of sight and travel alone, we want this to be as discreet as possible. Xzahi is a fair distance and I don't want this compromised by poor decision or off-handedness. Take this communicator so we can stay in touch and I can know of your progress, also, it enables you to directly put the one you eventually find, as the proposed leader, online to me. It may be difficult, there are so many factions that finding the one that will ally us may be awkward."

Tumi took hold of the written document and, without preparation, began his journey. Along the way, there are taverns, markets, and places he can camp if need be but he will travel at night as well, to make the journey a faster one. The flat board can take him to different heights, above the trees, and he's discovering much higher.

This helps prevent being seen, but also makes him vulnerable to predators such as the Zyu. Levitating through Kranaqus was one day but, in Akir, it is less tame, and the wildernesses overshadows the population and technology, so he has to be less carefree and more direct in his route to make it as short as possible and still avoid all compromising situations.

It took a day and a half to travel across Kranaqus, a half-day into Akir is when he noticed two black images following him. They were not small, and even though he felt he had not pushed the flat board to its limits and these black figures are fast.

It is a good thing that he brought the charging to unite with him, the flat board would not have been able to do the trip there and if he has to make it back it would have been on foot, or travelling beast, which is not very fast and he only has a few weeks before the announcement of the election. He then lowered himself so he was a hundred metres above the ground and sped up the board, as far as he knew no one has ever taken this thing this fast, he must be careful he'll be entering a forested area, and at this speed, he could easily be killed by a branch or an unknown obstacle unobserved by him.

Right now he only has the sands to concentrate on and, looking back, the black predators were not visible, so he believes he has outrun them. Crossing the inlet into Zed he began to realise, it took only one day to cross Akir on this when it, by regular travel devices, such as a beast or walking, it takes days or weeks depending on whether one stops to camp and rest or continue at a steady pace.

"*I must have been flying*," he thought to himself and started to snicker, "*of course I am, but who knew this device would have such an advantage over the normal travelling methods*."

Seeing that he was nearing the forests of Zed and the dunes were lessening in size. He slowed the board down to avoid injury.

As he entered the forest he thought to himself again, "*Maybe it would be better to travel above the trees so I can observe where the bigger camps are and where the biggest populations are located.*" with that consideration he raised to a higher altitude and brought himself above smoke escaping from a camp not far from where he started inside the forest.

It was not very large. Only a few hundred citizens, so he headed to Xzahi, which was his intention, to begin with, it is the largest known population and he knows they have the strongest governing faction in the province and, as well they travel the river in the northern route where it could carry the needed soldiers to ally Je-hu in the coup of the empire. The only problem is, who is in charge of this region and how does he get an audience with the leader.

Zed is not very well known, no one from Kranaqus has ever gone beyond the boards of Akir. Zeds army has held their own against Kranaqus. Mostly, because there are different governing camps on the borders and all over its territory, to any governing province, outside of Zed, this would be very confusing. But, in contradiction, it keeps the borders well-guarded and there are no orders needed from Xzahi to prevent Kranaqus from crossing into Zed and occupying land in its territory.

All of Zed is in conflict with who is in control of governing its borders and province. Each camp has its own ordinances of government handed down by tradition and birth rights. Each occupation or territory is itself a governing agent answering to no one. It's like gang warfare but each is its own act of law and government, putting at risk all citizens who travel between each territory without knowing where the borders begin or end, then, understanding each and every difference of freedoms inside each district and having the right papers and emblems to righteously pass through.

Hovering over top of the province of Zed the overall view was magnanimous, and breathe taking, but something uneventful started to happen, unexpectedly, arrows and streakers started tracing the skies around him so he started to ascend higher into the atmosphere. Streakers have a major distance but are unstable and have a short life and are not accurate, as they are part of the new technologies and haven't been worked with beyond experiment. As he climbed higher than he had ever been he was overwhelmed by the overall view and the number of fires throughout the province.

If he takes each formation as a different faction or order, then he can understand why there is so much chaos in the order of governing the province. But it makes it easier to decide which to involve or approach to aid in the assault on the estate. Tumi sees the river from the optimum height of three hundred metres and realises the best consideration would be to meet with one of the smaller communities, one nearest the river Ahi, at the mouth and offer the proposal to the governing bodies there.

It would be a faster depart and easier sail into the strait of Kaya, and less likely, a deception, or backstabbing, would occur when offered an alliance with Kranaqus. While soaring over the higher altitude Tumi discovered, on the banks of the Ahi River, a society with sailing ships, enough for at least two to be used as a means to transport five hundred soldiers. So he descended to further investigate who they are and what, if any, they are willing to include in this assault on the Kranaqus Empire.

Coming in from overhead he is seen by the whole town, including the head of the council. Tumi landed in the middle of the town square centre and was swamped by onlookers some started to bow, others began to ask questions.

"What are you?"

"Where do you come from?"

"Are you… a god?"

"I need to know, who holds the leadership of this town, and who is in charge of the shipyards and sailors," Tumi inquired, "Where do I go to find them."

"The person you are looking for is in the building just to our right in the middle of the courtyard, it has the markings of an Encarta tree. He lives in the house of council always and is there now." the elderly merchant pointed to a tall building, "His name is Lyaz, he will be able to bring together the ones to answer any questions you have about us."

Tumi got on the flat board and moved to the entrance and knocked on the front door, it is answered by an elderly looking gent who spoke softly, "yes, what can I do for you?"

Tumi looked at him and realised, this is the house, and said, "I am looking for Lyaz, is he in?"

"Just a minute and I'll see if he wishes to be seen at this time." he shut the door and Tumi waited for about twenty minutes before the sun came back what is it in regards to?" he questioned.

"I have just come down from the high valley and need to present a proposal of dire importance if I could see him for a moment it will become evident." the sub again shut the door and did not return for half an hour this time, when he returned he offered Tumi to enter and then showed him into a room with a large table and motioned him to sit, which he did.

"Lyaz will be with you momentarily, please be patient," and then left, while another entered who was obviously of military protocol, as he was heavily armed, though without a suit of armour he was still quite intimidating.

Tumi thought to himself, "*Well, we're getting closer to the source of who I need to speak to.*" but he still found himself sitting for another half hour before Lyaz came to the room and sat at the table but did not speak and also motioned for continued silence from Tumi.

Lyaz, a tall and assuming individual who believes much can be done without a lot of conversation, after a long period, about an hour Lyaz said, "You are the one who came out of the sky, yes?"

Tumi nodded.

"Are you with anyone?" continued Lyaz.

Tumi started to speak but was motioned to answer with a nod, and did so nodding yes.

"How do we address you?" Lyaz insisted.

"I am a representative of citizens against the committee of Kranaqus, so you can address me as you would any other in your hierarchy," Tumi replied with subtle intensity.

"Well," Lyaz interject, "It then appears we are on the same side, only you have a more intimate and direct connection to your contempt Gtzahi will be here momentarily he has this flying thing you arrived on, are there many? And how does one obtain such a device?"

"This is a new discovery, found only recently, and unknown to most, except to the governing powers and officials who keep records such as the archives, libraries, some of the generals have them for observation, and I've seen some military devices in use with this ability," Tumi explained, "They are very powerful and unstoppable making very little noise until put into striking action. The sound is that of a lightning strike and the action is ten times worse."

Just then a figure walked into the room and sat at the table.

"Aaa, councillor Gtzahi, we were just talking about devices, new to Kranaqus's military, please join us, I apologise but I did not introduce myself nor did I get your name before the conversation, you are," Tumi looked at them both and answered, "Tumi of Kranaqus, and you."

"I am Lyaz the town's administrative councillor and this is councillor Gtzahi, he controls the shipyards and their sailors and soldiers, when there is fighting to be considered. This happens quite frequently as we do control the mouth of the river and any who travel it are subject to our approval."

"We also have the first of three islands to the north the others are monitored by Akir but for the most part are isolated and independent from government interference. They rely on trade from us, and Akir and pay a small tax to Kranaqus to maintain independence." Gtzahi interjected a large aggressive and self-assured person, with facial scars who also walks with a limp.

“Then they have seen your ships frequent their waters and would not be suspicious to any convoy of three or four sailing through,” Tumi implied looking at the both of them with interest.

“No, as a matter of fact, we sail fleets of vestals through these waters without problems or interference from all that claim ownership of the surrounding lands and islands, the waters are neutral territory and trade is always done onshore with no tariffs or embargoes,” replied Gtzahi. “We have sailed fully armed vestals without confrontation but we are known for our ferocity when confronted and do not back down to fight.” he looked at Tumi with intensity, “What is your business and whom do you represent?”

Tumi sat back and grinned, “I am in need, we are a small group with a big plan that is in its final stage.” he stood up and walked to the window to overlook where the residence and he are, in the village, what his environment surrounding him is, turning he meets their eyes staring into his. He then began his explanation of what has occurred, to the point of needing help to infiltrate the estate, where the committee members hold their council.

“We need at least five hundred soldiers and four ships, they have already killed one of our MP’s who had decided to run for the Emperor’s seat and we feel that it is in our best interest to take over the committee’s involvement and create a whole new group action establishing a new committee membership and a better understanding of government for the people of Kranaqus.” Tumi gestured.

Gtzahi protested “What interest would it be of ours to get involved in such an undertaking we have all we need here and have no desire to create an enemy of such proportion or perhaps a war in which we would surely fail.”

Tumi then proceeded with, “There will be no war, we have an edge, one of the committee members is in our company and is giving us strategic support. This includes all the known entrances to the underground dungeons that lead to the heart of the estate. His name is Misric, have you heard of such a member?”

Gtzahi answered, “Yes, he is shrewd but also a mole, he hides well from conflict or confrontation, he and the committee have indirectly killed many of us here when confronted by their army. But, my question to you is, why did you not go to the largest Klan in the province Xzahi, to ally you in this confrontation? We have but maybe ten thousand worriers and that is only because of an alliance with five other clans along the beaches and up the river entering Xzahi. Would they have not been a better coalition with a greater force?”

Tumi went on to say, "Yes, that might be true but there is a downside to an alliance with such a large army. They are known for their deception and betrayal and we have not got time for such subversive intent. There is another factor at play and the one who can give knowledge to its relationship to this coup is at the ready to ally, and oversee all actions taken by our fusion."

Tumi continued, "You also have much to gain and Xzahi has little to offer except corruption. You will stay true as the mediation between Kranaqus and Zed. This gives you the upper hand of negotiation between the two provinces and guarantees a percentage in all activities of trade and or business. We must make haste a decision is needed as we only have several weeks to go into action and it takes a fleet of four at least five days to navigate the waters to Rox Island and the canal at Kaya is treacherous at the best of times and if a storm erupts the pass could be impossible." He looked at them in earnest, "before I introduce you to the citizen working with us I need an answer. This has to be done in the next few days, in reality, that is even too long be swift with your decision."

Lyaz interjected, "We shall conclude this meeting and resume with an answer tomorrow late in the day. I think to talk it over throughout the first part of the time unit we can come to an understanding and decision and will present it in the later hour of the day. Leave us and be back here after the late meal."

Chapter 29
The Point

The point
Is
What you
Want to think
Is where
You want to
Take your mind
Is what you read in ink

The point
Is
What you
Want to know
Is what
What your mind
Is telling you
And where you
Think you'll go

The point
Is
Where you go
From here
Is what
Your friend
Is telling you
And what you think is clear
What we have
Or have not
Is this or
Is this not
The point
You meet me
I see you
Midnight rendezvous
At the point

The following day Tumi showed, on time, but had to wait until Lyaz and Gtzahi were ready to make an appearance. That was at least one hour or more, but his patience paid off as they showed with surprisingly good news, as they entered the communications room Lyaz hinted that they are going to accept his request but they should sit and go over what is written. “So, have you brought anything for us to read?” Lyaz asked with disdain.

“Yes, but, before it can be given I need to know what your decision is,” Tumi replied with suspicion.

“And what if we have none,” answered Lyaz.

“Then, I will move on to the next Klan and ask for their support with an alliance, and when you discover what riches they have from such a coalition you will realise the opportunity you had and let pass due to your own paranoid reluctance, and just to let you know the next stop is Xzahi. So you can be the one who holds all the cards or…” Tumi gave them time to consider and interject with their decision.

“Don’t be so quick to dismiss us; we just wanted to know what you had as an alternate. We have agreed to accept your proposal and would like to know how you came to choose us as an alliance,” Gtzahi inquired.

“It was just a thought or a split-second strategic decision you have control of the river’s mouth and, we know that Xzahi has the largest army inside Zed. Strategically, would it not be better to ally ourselves with a smaller company of warriors who would be more resourceful and be looking for a way to strengthen their place in this region by having an ally of great power, rather than be overwhelmed by a great army who could turn this coup upside down, taking everything and not have any consideration to the negotiation of treaties or diplomatic alliances for future advancement for all citizens on Qua. Such as the flat board I rode in on.” Tumi gestured to the board sitting out in the yard being observed by some of the staff members to, the house of Lyaz.

“Good judgment, but what makes you so sure we would not have a similar plan of deceit.” Questioned Lyaz, “You are too smart not to want to assure your place with such a fusion, strengthening your forces here, rather than dealing with the uncertainty of conquest. These things are always risky and can become mutinous or backfire completely, leaving you than with nothing.”

“All right, all right, we concede and know you are right. We would like to read what you have.”

"You're going to have to wait. Before I expose anything to you there is someone you need to talk to." Tumi pulled out his communicator and opened it Je-hu was immediately brought up and the two, Lyaz and Gtzahi, looked into it and gasped, "Is that real?" demanded Gtzahi.

"What is this evil? This glass piece seems very suspicious how can we believe what we're looking at." just at that moment Je-hu entered the room and interjected, "Because we offer truths, not fabrication." Tumi was so startled he threw the communicator into the air and fell backwards off his chair.

"How do you do that, it freaks me every, time how fast do these flat boards move anyway?" Tumi asked in astonishment.

"I'm not going to be here long and, I want you to stay with the envoy as they make their way to the landing zone. How long do you think it will take before you arrive?"

"We have a map so we can show the travel route?"

"I can show you an actual visual of the planet and you can show us the best and fastest path to get to the Island Rox." Je-hu told the trio and opening his communicator he brought up his visual of the land formations and coastal shorelines. Je-hu punched in some codes and the Qua landforms came on screen he then punched in another code and printed, on a tabled piece of paper the images of Qua, the half side where the landforms of the states and provinces lay.

Giving it to Tumi, Lyaz and he stood over it and laid out the voyage the ships will take to get to the shores of Rox.

"This journey will take nine days," exclaimed Gtzahi. "And that is relying on the weather. If there are storms it will be longer but, this is not the time for that we must prepare. It will take a few days to gather enough worriers and make ready each ship Tumi can keep you informed on the departure time so you can stand by on the arrival date," assured Gtzahi.

"Good, I'll return to Rox and inform them of your alliance and work out the strategy with the rest of the team Misric has assured us of his knowledge and we can rely on his full cooperation." Je-hu gestured to Tumi to walk with him. "Our time is short; we must have these troops on the shores no later than eighteen days from tomorrow. These people cannot be trusted, have they signed the agreement?" inquired Je-hu.

"No, I haven't let them read it yet. I will do so after you leave but I question their loyalty the shortness of time is on our side, this cannot be successful without them, and within the time frame of this period, set by the committee."

Tumi said with hesitation, "I'll go back in and get them to read and sign the agreement, but should they want to add anything what do I do, agree to everything they demand or check in with you?"

"Put down at the top of the additions to be disused, and let them know that everything added is not solid until met with me and voted on by the new committee," Je-hu insisted. He then turned and started walking towards the road as though he had hidden his board behind a hillside. Tumi walked back into the house and presented the agreement to the waiting allies. Je-hu jumped back to the beach where the others were waiting, of course, he had to walk a distance as he could not let anyone know of this advanced tech they can only be a part of what they know to exist in their own discoveries and known advancements, anything more would be a deviation.

Preparing for the voyage was swift. Getting five hundred warriors was not difficult. Because Gtzahi has allied his clan with others along the beaches and the interior of Zed, bringing together an alliance of warriors formed quickly. Separating them between the four vestals went smooth.

When it was told what the campaign is, no one disrupted the flow of the system of rules. They would make two port stops along the way, to dispose of any suspicion and to look like merchant ships. They would do some trading and bartering just to maintain authenticity.

It would take six days, with stops, to reach the cavern at Kayas caves. Just before they arrived, one day out, a two-planet eclipse started, this is bad. Single eclipses can be treacherous but a double eclipse is disastrous. A single eclipse causes first, darkness, darkness is rare, there is no artificial lighting on the waters and navigating the cavern is difficult in the best light.

In this narrow passage, the waters are turbulent and pulsating, only the best captains dare to contemplate such a challenge, and most sail around the tip of Xyph to reach Kranaqus, but the cavern saves four days of travel if executed successfully. Second, during an eclipse where the shadow of the planet falls is always in question and where it happens there is always confusion, and in this instance, it fell upon the cavern. The trouble with a double eclipse is it lasts twice as long.

As they approached the cavern the turbulence of the ocean began to get stronger.

There is another cause of a double eclipse. Because the orbits of the planets are erratic the distance of the planets vary, and the gravitational pull of both planets creates a greater pull on the two moons, and this, in turn, makes the tidal flow higher and the currents stronger, causing the passage through the cavern to become more treacherous. At the time of their arrival at the cave entrance, the four ships got caught in the pull of the current and were dragged into the cavern with no control.

Most of the turbulence was centred through the narrow passage and that gave Gtzahi an idea, the high waters created a tsunami-like wave through the cavern, signalling to Tumi. “alert the other vessels let them know to lower their aft and mid sails and to steer their ships into the centre of the cavern,” Gtzahi directed Tumi, having more control on his flat-board then the water-bearing vessels, “also let them know to stay at least five hundred metres aft of each other so there is no chance of collision.”

Entrance to the cavern, for the vessels to carry between the cavern walls, had to be central as they poised each ship into the mouth and when the current caught them it swept each one into the centre.

The speed was faster than any had ever sailed, but it soon became apparent that the winds within the cavern would carry them through without incident, the sails would have to be dropped immediately once clear, or they could be swept into the coral reefs on the other side.

They all made it through with few casualties while bringing down the sails before clearing the cavern, several of the men were blown off the bow, the turbulence made it impossible to save any of them, in all, five were lost. It didn’t reduce the strength of the company but had an impact on the rest of the men. These warriors are very superstitious and any negative can imply a bad omen and change the outcome of any campaign or plan before acting upon it.

Chapter 30
Welcome

Welcome to my prison
It's where I remain
Here I sit in a clay dream
Surrounded by the insane
As you roll around in time
Could it be you're quite like me
Just somewhere out of mind

Sometimes I'm a drifter
No money for a ride
Where to go when
To get there
There's no other side
No other side

What is your hurry
As you drift there
Where to go
In my nightmare
It's all happening again

Welcome to my prison
Cell 124
Here I sit in a clay dream
With hundreds on my floor

Roaches around the floor hole
Yet I can endure
So as you ponder
The thought and wander
Where do you draw the line
The sunny side of heaven
While waiting around to die

While Tumi was making his way to Zed in search of an ally Je-hu directed Naveen to separate Misric from the others and restrain him in a side area. "You were very helpful with the floor plans inside the estate, but now, we need the exits. And I'm not talking about the visible ones. We need the hidden emergency exits beneath the estate." demanded Je-hu, "you gave an excellent diagram of the inner floor plans, but not the whole lower level, it doesn't have to be to scale just a visual exterior layout and wherein the estate they enter."

Naveen looking at Je-hu then interjected with, "We also need to know the depth of the lower levels how deep into the ground they go and the capacity of space and the way to the main floor. If there are any hidden passages throughout the, that lead into main rooms, conference rooms, halls and so on. Then we need to know that as well. Don't make us use force, because it won't be what you think."

Misric, looking over the area, saw a table with the layouts he drew for Je-hu, walking over he sat down and began to do an over view of what he had exposed, and felt only redemption for trying to kill him and, yes, the directions were perfect. "*He, he, he, he, he, ha, ha, ha, they are going to be shocked when they see me. You red ires, try to kill me hey, I'll be making pate of their brains after this.*" He thought to himself.

The exterior layout of the estate, including the grounds and beyond the outer edge, of the fenced area, "I have gone beyond the fencing, because, all the exit points are on the outside of them. It wouldn't be smart to have points of egress just to have to climb fencing once on the outside."

Misric expressed, looking up at Naveen, "I have also included where the start in the building and the red lines between the walls are hidden passages the entrances in green and the exits in blue, the numbers are the floors they are on, and since it is a villa, I have included where the committee members are housed."

Je-hu gathered the team together to meet at the landing at the beach. He first met with Tumi, "How was the passage?" He inquired.

"Treacherous, we lost five," Tumi said with a hint of sadness.

"Oh, we'll have an oration; in the meantime, we can go over the layout Misric made. It seems you have the men divided into four divisions so there won't be a question of placement."

Je-hu gave a quick glance at the ships at anchor offshore, "We have six exit points, what we need now is some inside info. What is going on with their armies? How many troops are in the city? What kind of guarding is in the house right now? And have there been any leaks to the committee about this?"

"We still have our spies in the estate and can find out what they have been hearing to date." Tumi started to move towards the flat board and got ready to make his way to the estate, "Yasir is still in with the ground's security and can still be contacted. It will take me a few days to get the word out and arrange for a meeting, we still have several weeks before the preliminary speeches, let's plan for the week before opening and make sure there are no snags." Tumi got on his board and flew off over the treetops towards Rox.

As he drew closer to Rox he began to notice heavy security. Surrounding the estate is a legion of soldiers, "*This is going to be tricky,*" he thought to himself.

It seemed as though the committee had anticipated some kind of action and reinforced the city with most of the armies' soldiers.

"Getting to Yasir is going to prove difficult; I'm going to have to resort to a stealthier tactic."

He grounded himself outside Rox and chose to walk to where he might meet up with some of the inside team. Sora was not there but he knows the residence of all the team members and figured he would have to check each one to get an idea of what is going on. Yasir, being a guard inside the estate resides inside. The only way to get to him is to arrange a meeting through kitchen staff or janitorial.

As he rounded the corner to Nehan's place he almost bumped into the guard standing at the edge of the building. "*Say nothing,*" he whispered and walked past without looking at anyone. Hoping Nehan or the team has not been discovered he made his way to Raju, all was clear, but he also was not home. Deciding to wait he went over to a nearby tavern and ordered some food and drink.

Making his way back to Raju's, after a few hours had rolled by, he saw, this time, there is a light on and walked up to the door. Knocking a voice came from behind it, "Say who you are or I will shoot through the door" Raju's voice was shaky yet stern.

"It is I Tumi, I need to talk," the door opened a crack, just to be able to peer out, "I need to know if you are Tumi before letting you in, you look like him but I need proof." Tumi took out his registration tags and handed them to Raju He then opened the door just enough for Tumi to slip inside.

"I do apologise for my caution but there is great unrest as we near the openings of the election. Some of the team, as you know, has been discovered and I must maintain a high suspicion of all who come to my door."

"Understandable, but I am here in need of meeting with Yasir, do you still have access to him or is everything in lockdown?"

"I'm only a janitor, so the information I have is limited to hearsay and speculation. What I can do, as a janitor, I have access to every room and area in the estate, is get in touch with Yasir and set up a meet where he could pass some information to you through me."

"That would be that would be important what we need to know is, guard postings, how many troops are on the grounds at any given time, the weakest point of entry, and how much of the estate is guarded, inside, at any given time." Tumi wrote all the questions down and handed them to Raju.

"The last I heard from him is he was to be promoted to the supervision of the inner core, which means, he will be hard to trace. But as I said I have access. So, just by wandering around, I can stumble into his quarters and set up transactions between the two of us."

"Is there any of us left in the kitchen?"

"Yes, Nehan."

"I strode past his place before coming here it was heavily guarded, do you have any idea what that is about?"

"No. As I said the info we get is usually second hand and cannot be reliable. But once I vantage a correspondence with Yasir the information will be more certain, If he is still in the loop. We cannot be sure."

"Yes, we must be cautious." Raju went to the fridge and served both of them beverages. "It has been several weeks since we have heard from Yasir so we must be ready for betrayal, When can you get back to me?" Tumi asked.

"I'm at the estate; once I find out where he is I can begin a messaging hand off," Raju exclaimed.

"We have a very limited time and need to know what to expect before our penetration of the estate."

"Three days, we meet back here."

"OK, same time or later."

"Make it later; I don't get off until mid-day and I want to relax before your arrival. Plus there is less activity on the streets and you are less likely to be observed."

"Great, late afternoon then."

The next morning Raju went to the Estate and, without hesitation, proceeded to the main office of the "guards and securities" and asked about Yasir. He arranged to have a meeting with him, it wasn't out of character, the janitors and guards often communicated; after all, they are the only departments that have access to all areas and generally know what's going on in the building. After leaving a message he went about his duties.

That afternoon he requested to the securities office where Yasir was waiting, "Hey Raj."

"Hey, I was wondering if we could meet for a drink later."

"Sure, it'll have to be outside the estate, if that's all right."

"Ya, what time are you free?"

"How about eight, at the spears tavern, the one around the corner from your place."

"Ya, eight then."

* * *

Raju was off at four and got there early and was sitting in the corner of the tavern when Yasir arrived, he seated himself and ordered a brew, "It's been a few weeks, how have you been?"

"Busy, there is much to discuss, but it is best we show a good time and prepare messages to be passed in the Estate." They sat and talked of past times and brighter futures with jokes and sarcasm, and after a few hours, Raju passes a container they departed home and to the estate. When opened late in the hour Yasir found a layout of the estate and grounds, to expose the greater forces of guards and soldiers times and placement of rounds and unite camps.

It is easy to pass messages to Raju, by tossing them as garbage; it is retrievable during the collection and dumping in the dungeons of the lower levels or the outer stables. He got what he needed for Tumi and proceeded to make arrangements to see him.

"Can Yasir be trusted after all this time?" Tumi questioned.

"I don't know, he seemed genuine, but deception is a tricky game and we can only be suspicious of the swiftness of this information and how quickly he has been promoted." Raju' looking at Naveen and Je-hu standing in front of him, Tumi was off with the other warriors making decisions on who to include and how many.

"That is suspicious," Je-hu said, "we have to take precautions and that means we enter in fewer numbers and in three different times. There are six entrances, we will only use five, one will be left for reinforcements or a quick escape. Raju> was there any mention by you about the secret entrances to the estate?" Je-hu inquired.

"No, but I have made arrangements to meet with him in a few days, if I don't return you know then that his information is an act of deception, yet, I have not given our means of approach or entering the yard. Also, he does not have the time factor and we can use deception for this occurrence as well." Raju, for a janitor, was acting like a strategist and his understanding of deceit shows a history of it. Most likely in his relationships, but that knowledge works on every level of interaction of lives interchanges and practices in social and corporate affairs. And in this moment of attainment, it is extremely useful.

Looking at the layout and time changes for securities and groupings of the armies, they don't have any that are set around the exterior of the estate yard which is an oversight on the behalf of the committee. But, communication between the Generals, Admirals, and committee members is strained, and the planning of yard layout is often left to the generals who tend to want to be as close to the facility as possible, so there are no camps outside the estate yard, and only two of the secret escape exits are compromised.

That leaves four for easy access and one questionable. But two could leave for a quick escape, if things go awry and we can send in eight teams of ten that will attack at different intervals, into different parts of the estate. There are three levels beneath the Emperors estate and each of the levels has two escape routes, unknown to everyone but the committee and the head of the securities.

Je-hu was in a complete moment of elation, with unknown consideration to whom he had involved and organised into a team.

They have brought together a winning plot to begin a new epoch.

We know where the committee members and their selected MG's, for the campaign to the Emperor's seat, are hold up but between them and us are a mass of soldiers and guards.

Chapter 31
The Defeat

"The plan is set," Je-hu began to explain. "Misric has plotted all the secret exits and they are all known, with the markings, how to find them with ease, so there will be no guessing or confusion. The first team assault will be from the level under the main floor, they start to make preparations and bring together the teams for the first assault.

"Every assault unit has a communicator so it's known where they each are and what their status is. There are four other assault teams, each one will enter at the same time, ten minutes after the first team enters the upper tunnel. Its entrance is near the kitchen leading to the main floor, hidden by a panel. The panel blends with the wall so to find it one has to know where the latch, to open it, is located in the corner of the kitchen."

Je-hu, pointing out each area as he continued to give details for each commander to follow, "The outside exits are marked, when looking around one must be aware of the plants and growth surrounding the area on the ground and the fencing. Because the porthole is camouflaged by dirt and overgrowth the markings are very important otherwise one could be looking for days. Misric is very clear on the way it is set and how to detect each one. The hatches are steel so a magnetometer is the best source of detection. We have only three."

Then Tumi interjected with, "We have disused the assault with great detail and believe that we have to cover all sources of entry, but the first assault will come from the first lower level, there will be two parties.

"Each level has two tunnels to the outer yards beyond the ramparts. Each team, of the first assault, will have no more than ten men. This will limit the losses and establish a front. When the second wave enters there will be reinforcement of forty men, twenty to each team, the same with the third making each assault, a reinforcement to the other, and a harder force to be opposed.

“We are to assume that the majority of the armies will be outside and, after locking the doors from the inside, it will be near impossible to counter our attack.” Tumi included, “There must be a distraction while entering the tunnels.

Of five hundred, we will use one hundred to enter the escape routes. For the first two entries, teams often, for the second of two entries teams of twenty and the same with the third. The other four hundred will maintain the distraction in two waves; they will both lead from the front gated entrance.

“The first will attack as the two upper teams enter the chambers. This level is an open area meant for the storage of produce and valuables. The entrance to this level is parallel to the stairwell once inside and on the floor, it has easy access into the estate, it shouldn’t take more than twenty minutes to make their way to the main floor of the state. The first assault will give them enough time to achieve this.” Tumi concluded.

On the communicators, the first wave of one hundred at the front gate arrives with no complication. Large masses of travel units are always expected on election campaigning, spreading out to appear, not as an army, as viewing audience and merchants along with the campaigning that will begin within the next week. Hidden in their carts and trailers, some of the mercenaries are using flat boards, are the heavy artillery and weapons.

Every resource will accompany each wave, and with them, new tech devices scrounged by the dark market at Misric’s intelligence leading the second wave to where they are located and how the storage could be compromised quickly, without being observed.

“Stompers and blinders, coupled with pressurizer grenades, black hole disruptor, will be distributed between the second and third wave of attack. These weapons are still fresh and, for the most part, untested in battle. So it’s questionable how they will affect the area and the damage they will cause. There have only been small tests In Laboratories so Je-hu has told all the leaders of each wave to be cautious and selective,” said Tumi.

“There is to be no unnecessary deaths or damages due to overzealousness. We have surprise on our side and the Intel of one of the committee members, so, with his description of the working finished products, you must take caution and be very careful. There is much at stake and everyone should be able to return in good shape the only suffering should be with the opposition. We take no prisoners and we hold all accountable for the past persecution. By sending the first wave with minimal and obsolete weaponry, and by surprising them with their own new resources, we will gain the upper hand and allow the assault on the Estate to go in undetected."

Tumi went on with, "This engagement should not be more than two or three hours before the second wave arrives. The campaign should only last days, if it takes more time than that we are lost and will have to retreat. This should not be an option. We will be successful as we have the element of surprise on our side."

Still looking at the entourage he continued, "No one shall speak, no one will make reference, silence is our only ally at this time."

Stepping away from the faces of exuberance he motioned to the first hundred fifty to begin the first wave, and the one hundred who are dropping into the tunnels, to leave now as it will take two days' time to travel from where they are holding up. The second and third waves will take foot the following day and will break into the storage where the weapons are being held.

"From what has been observed most of the armies are at the Estate and preparing for the campaigning of the Emperor's seat." Je-hu had taken the generals aside to remind them of the heightened securities around the estate and that suspicious behaviour would be easily detected, "So get in and stake your ground as quickly as possible, the higher the territory the better the position, you are all professionals and it should take less than an hour."

Je-hu motioned, "The estate is built in a valley, there was no forethought to this placement, other than the fact that it sits above a cavern with an endless pit at the bottom, created by an aquifer deep in the ground. This gave an excellent lower dungeon of three levels with more pending. The levels have a ceiling height of six metres that are accessible from the main floor of the Estate.

"To get to the bottom of the cavern, a crude staircase was built but the invention of flat board technologies, it rendered its use obsolete. At the bottom of the cavern is a well-like structure, with a three-metre radius. This fissure was also created by a natural aquifer, where most of the water is gotten by the peoples because the aquifer runs through the whole continent and is the largest resource of fresh water, wells are the major resource of how water is gotten except where there is pumping available which only exists in urban areas or where it is forded by rural municipalities, which are minimal.

"The tunnels are on each level, two to each, and except for the upper two on level one, are open entrances." Je-hu, looking at Tumi, motioned him to give further information,

Tumi added, “The hills and high peaks of the surrounding mountains are where the artillery storage compounds are. The reason being, they are better defended that way and less likely to be compromised by enemy forces. So the guards, during an election, are not so tight and Misric has given easy access to the most important one where all the new armaments are created and stored.

“The new technologies are not widely known so it is not guarded heavily, especially since Rox is an island and most of the time well stationed with centurions, except at election times. As the committee begins election preparations they are very paranoid about their safety.

“The cavern is so large one would think that the weapons silos and technologies would be placed in it, but paranoia again set in, and an alternate placement for such undertakings was found in the surrounding terrain. Being in a valley the city is surrounded by hills and mountains on both sides, Rox city extends to the shoreline on the west coast of the Island of Rox on the beach, where the valley ends.

“The escape exits form a pyramid when creating a line from the centre of each cover. The first to be entered will lead to the first level, and then the other four will follow. They should maintain a fifteen-minute difference between the three teams after meeting on the levels the tunnels open onto. They will reinforce the attacking party in a sequence of fifteen-minute intervals, when they clash together inside it will give the illusion of a greater force.”

The outer militants were starting to claim their ground on the hills to the left and right of the Estate, which is set on a hill fifteen metres above the valley floor. It lay between two mountains, the one to the south is 450 metres high, and the one to the north is 380 metres high. The silo to the north of the Estate is the one the second wave of the first party will enter, using the hidden tunnel plotted by Misric, so the exact location and how to compromise its entrance was given to them.

Each wave of both operations was given communicators, when each was set in position there would be conformation and they would know what is happening above and below the grounds of the estate.

The first wave, in front of the Estate, is ready and waiting for the reinforcements to verify their position and the success of their incursion. Leader two acknowledged that they have just exited the silo and they are a half days’ time away.

If they opened up now the second wave would be there just as the first team entered the first level to the estate.

That's when the first cannon blasts were heard by the leadership team, as they reached level one, under the estate the third and second teams entered the tunnels to the two bottom levels. There was no resistance on the first level; all the guards and soldiers were at the front gates defending the grounds. The plan is taking on the right execution, just as expected, as the other two teams were on the two lower levels team one had entered the estate and were already searching for the committee members.

When they reached the kitchen in the villa it was empty, they could only assume everyone had evacuated but where? They began to pan out into the kitchen and at each end were an exit one top the courtyard the other to the offices. When they got to the thresholds looking out they could see at the front of the courtyard the armies were stationed in the first office, with three guards posted, taking positions at both the second team arrived and quickly scuttled up to the second floor resuming stealth disquiet.

On the second floor, they began entering the townhouses and lower offices and taking positions surrounding the officers in the first lower business office, while the third team stationed themselves in the kitchen.

From what they could observe there were no more than eight officers in the room and three posted guards, on the outside, soldiers were barricaded around the outer perimeter and scuffling to reach other positions in to fend off the oncoming Militia.

That's when the first team leader yelled, "HEY, you are all surrounded put down your weapons!" as that was being forwarded the three guards raised their weapons and opened fire, and even though their armaments were higher tech they were outnumbered and outgunned and easily overtaken. The officers inside the room quickly surrendered and the teams fanned out on each floor in search of the committee members.

Locking the glass entrance to the courtyard the three leaders sent out one officer and forced the armies to stand down and let the Militia step in unharmed. They finally found the committee members in the archives above the offices on the sixth floor. The room was a safe room for just an event so they would be out of reach and out of sight until the fighting ended.

Then they could emerge unharmed and continue on without delay. It just so happens that this time their army was overrun and they emerged into the hands of the militia.

"Well, this is an uncompromising circumstance, is it not?" said Tumi looking at each one of the members.

Yasir, walking up behind Tumi, staring at the committee exclaimed, "Tumi, I've been waiting patiently for this moment, I put myself on guard here hoping for this outcome."

"Where is Je-hu?" he asked shrugging his shoulders.

"He won't be here and has given me specific instructions to follow once we have overtaken the Empire, but first I have some introductions to make."

Turning to the committee members Tumi began, "I suppose you're wondering how this happened and so fast. There is someone I would like you to meet." Tumi motioned to one of the leaders to bring the citizen forward, "I do believe you know who this is, right?" they all looked on in astonishment mouthing, "*Misric*"

"You're dead," Fanyrottiss insisted.

"Obviously, I am not," he replied.

"How?" Fanyrottiss questioned.

And Naveen answered the question short and to the point, ending with, "Sometimes an adversary can play a major part in the outcome of a confrontation when they themselves have been spared."

"Take these three to the lower dungeons, Yasir, accompany them to make sure they don't escape. There are too many secrets in this place to trust that they will stay in their compounds for very long, separate them and chain them, their fate is already written, and it's just a matter of time."

"You cannot do this! You have no rights here. You are unknowns. What makes you think that you will get away with this?" Ayxan said intensely.

Chapter 32
A New Order

To Question

You've got vampire eye's
But wear a werewolf disguise
You smile with simple sighs
And hold the mask of a devil

You see with night light red
But live in day light instead
You shoot in black and white
Death in colour just ain't right

You're like a shower in the rain
Or a snow fall on a summers day
The tracks simply melt away
Later someone else will pay

You spread yourself around
And feed on all that you see
Cause you're the first to come down
Filled with last nights mysteries

Is it easier to question
or answer her in vain
is it better to play it
or learn how to play
The game

After handling the committee members Tumi, Naveen, Je-hu, Yasir, Zavita, Sora, Nayrr, Lyaz and Esyr, sat down at the table, in the kitchen and began the arduous work of change.

"Where to start," Je-hu looked around the table and motioned Zavita to stand, "I do not want to influence much here, there are two things that need to be put into effect immediately without question." pausing he looked over the table of faces and began again, "Zavita, you are the only choice for the adjustment of who will sit as Emperor.

"You are the face of change and the voice of diplomacy. All at this table have an interest in the future of the survival of this world, this solar system. Without the placement of the web on all celestial bodies, we will all perish.

"I also want to make a change in the number of committee members. Seven will be the new membership and I believe we have that with the complement of citizens before me. As a member Lyaz, you are the ambassador to Zed. The rest of you know very well what and where the wrongness lay in the order of law and business. An alliance with Zed will prove to be of great value."

After the apprehension of the committee and the seizure of the estate members and staff, as well as their expected campaign non-appointed subordinates, to our dismay, they did not stand down without a fight. We had overwhelmed the armies by surprising them within the estate and, not being ready for such an intervention; the battle was won in half a day.

Now we can complete

The Web

Planet Qua

The Strategy

To begin placement of the obelisks, monoliths, megaliths, all of these words apply. This prevents confusion and gives the process a deeper meaning.